Novice Mystery - Ireland

The First Dan and Karen Novice Mystery

Donna Rewolinski

Orange Hat Publishing
www.orangehatpublishing.com - Waukesha, WI

Novice Mystery - Ireland by Donna Rewolinski
ISBN 978-1-948365-40-6

For information, please contact:

Orange Hat Publishing
603 N Grand Ave.
Waukesha, WI 53186
www.orangehatpublishing.com

Edited by Denise Guibord
Cover design by Tom Heffron

www.orangehatpublishing.com

I wish to thank my husband, Frank, for his loving support, inspiration and technical contributions. I would also like to thank Holly Schoenecker for her early editing and Judy Bridges, Robert Vaughan, Kim Suhr and members of the Redbird/Red Oak Thursday night Writer's Roundtable Critique group that helped me hone this book along the way.

Chapter 1

There's a small hand patting my arm during the continuation of Karen's speech. I have it memorized, so while she talks, I watch the airport, the plane, think about suspicious travelers, and—

". . . put up with years of you working through the weekend, being called out in the middle of the night, missing holidays and celebrations. I love you to death, but I'm ready for our plans not to be in constant risk of disruption. We didn't live like other people." At my raised eyebrows, Karen backtracks, "Okay, we didn't live the way people *think* ordinary people live. And now we've landed in Dublin, think of this as your payback to me, for not getting shot. *Are* you paying attention?"

Cocking my head to the side, "I thought *I* was your payback."

In a familiar gesture that could be a caress, but is more a squeeze on my chin, just a bit too tight. "Idiot. Of course. Okay, look on this as a *reward* for me."

"For?"

"For putting up with thirty-one years of midnight phone calls, squashed cockroaches on the bottom of your shoes, regulation haircuts, and—"

"I thought you liked my hair short and professional."

"Yes, I do. I think you're missing the point," Karen says. Her eyes search mine, "Are you having second thoughts about this vacation?"

I put my hands up, "No, no. I'm not having second thoughts. It's an 'aventure.'" I wink.

Karen lowers her shoulders and smiles, "I haven't heard that expression since Eric was four or five years old."

Almost thirty years ago when I was a patrol officer, our son, Eric couldn't say adventure, so 'aventure' is anything new and exciting. These upcoming three months in a place we've dreamed about for many years—Ireland will be 'aventure.'

Airports in Ireland smell the same as airports anywhere. It's a combination of old sweat, rubber, and someone wearing too much cologne. We snake our way through the custom's line. While we wait, I glance at my passport. I'm not sure our photos do us justice, but does anyone's? I think I'm looking okay for my age. I have all my hair, I'm tall enough at 6'1" and carry more weight than I'd like. I hope I'd still make the mile in regulation time, bad knees and all. The young customs officer questions us, mostly me, "So Detective Daniel Novice, what's the nature of your trip to Ireland?"

"Pleasure. I retired from law enforcement and this is the reward for my wife and me."

"Are you carrying a gun?" No humor, all business. Frown included free of charge. This guy isn't impressed by American law enforcement.

"No."

"Are you aware of Ireland's gun laws?"

"Yes."

"How long do you plan to stay in Ireland?"

"Three months."

"Where are you staying?'

"The village of Ballyram."

The customs agent appears to relax somewhat as his shoulders reset themselves and his frown uncurls—slightly. He turns his attention to Karen. She's five inches shorter than I am with reddish shoulder-length hair and a pretty face. She's a retired social worker with a deep intuition. At times, she has an eerily perceptive insight into people and situations. I've often told her that she should have been the detective in the family. She'd state, "I would, except I don't do blood, bodily fluids, people yelling at me, or autopsy.

"This picture doesn't look like you," the agent remarks.

Karen shrugs, "I was eight years younger, thirty pounds lighter, and my hair was a different color in that picture."

The customs agent nods and stamps our passports. We're officially in Ireland!

Walking a safe distance from the customs agent, Karen laughs, "What did he mean, 'This picture doesn't look like you.' Did he think it was a forgery? I was attempted to tell him, 'Since completing my international terrorist training, I was forced to reinvent my look.' But that probably wouldn't have gone over well."

All those years of police training send sweat prickles along my spine and makes the hair at the back of my neck stand upright. "Definitely wouldn't have gone over well. Thank you for not saying it."

We make our way to the luggage carousel and gratefully all ours has arrived. We follow signage to the car rental agency in the basement of the airport. Our attendant copies our U.S. driver's license, provides us a short tutorial on how the car's navigational system works, uses his head, his finger, and his voice to direct us toward the bank of rentals in the airport parking garage.

Karen smiles when she sees the car, "It's nice. I think it's a good size if we have more adults than just you and me. It's weird to see the steering wheel on the right side of the car."

I start, "It's a—"

Karen stops me, "I don't know cars, even if you tell me. I know it's black and has four doors. I'm good with that."

"Okay."

Karen nods in agreement, "Can you set Bridget for Ballyram?"

"Bridget? You already named our Irish navigational system 'Bridget.' Why?"

Karen looks at me sideways, "Because I sat next to a cute older woman on the plane. She was returning home to Ireland and she was a joy to talk to. She loves Americans and wishes us nothing but the best during our time here."

"Why don't I remember seeing you talk to her?"

"Because you fell asleep the minute the plane was in the air and didn't wake up until we were about to land."

"Okay. Well, then, Bridget it is!"

Dublin behind us, I'm struck by the beauty of this country. I don't know who first described Ireland as, 'The forty shades of green,' but it's true. I see the pastures, trees and shrubs that border fields are a blend of greens, tans, browns and yellow. But overall, I see green, a soothing, moist, welcoming green.

"The roads are a bit narrow," I comment. They're paved but driving these twists and turns at a speed of 80-100 kilometers, which is our American 55-65 miles per hour, is admittedly a little stressful.

“Watch out for the trees,” Karen points. “The guidebook said the country lanes would be narrow, but I wasn’t expecting the trees to be so close to the road—right next to the road. You think they trim the trees, or let the vehicles do it?”

I don’t answer; I’m concentrating. It’s still unnerving that we’re on the ‘wrong’ side of the road. And we’re constantly coming up on another roundabout or to the Irish, ‘a turning circle.’

“What’s with all the roundabouts?” Karen asks, apparently reading my mind, “There seems to be one every few miles. I don’t think we have more than five or six in the entire county back home. Why are there so many here?”

Using my professional, police officer voice, “Do you know that roundabouts are statistically safer than having an entrance and exit ramp. Traffic in the circle has the right of way and entering traffic needs to slow down and be aware of oncoming traffic.”

Mockingly, Karen states, “No, I did not know that. Wow, I thought you retired and left your coppy sense back in the States.”

Winking at Karen, “You know, if I had feelings, they would be hurt. I have experience with roundabouts. While in the army, I was stationed in Europe and they had roundabouts at that time.”

“Just as long as you know what you’re doing. How do you know what lane to get into so you can exit when you want?”

“I’m a professional! Trust me.” At which point I make an assertive lane change because I am in the wrong lane when my exit comes up. Luckily, oncoming traffic was on my side of the car and Karen doesn’t have a direct line of slight. Upon exiting the roundabout, I hear Karen yelling and pointing, “Other side, other side.” I was driving into oncoming traffic, but I adeptly swerve into the correct lane, “See, I’m a professional, like I said.”

Karen stifles a laugh and gazes out the side window, "This place is beautiful. The hills and fields roll down into the slate grey walls. I heard that Ireland has rocky soil. I guess when you have rocks you build rock walls. I love how the vines climb over the walls. It just feels magical. Like anything could happen. I can picture fairies dancing in the woods or spirits haunting castle ruins. I'm glad we're here."

"Me, too. A pot of gold at the end of a rainbow wouldn't hurt, though."

"True, but for now we're two retired people on vacation, right?" Karen reminds me.

"Yup." It's a promise, if promises are made in hope and not in belief.

Several hours later, we arrive in Ballyram. Karen and I hope that our research finds this village a great mix of small town life, city amenities near tourist attractions, and local entertainment and dining. We find the real estate office. While Karen waits in the car, I go in and meet an office staff member who is dressed in brown and put on her bland-face today.

"Hi, I'm Dan Novice. I'm here to pick up the keys to our cottage."

Suddenly a voiced is raised, "Dan Novice?"

I'm bewildered as I can't see who the voice belongs to. "Yes," I hesitantly reply.

A man appears from a back office. He looks like Elvis. That's if Elvis were no more than five feet tall, in his mid-forties, close to two-hundred pounds, and had an Irish accent.

He extends his hand, "I'm John Shea." I notice there's a gold ring on each finger, one a lion head. His partially open dress shirt

reveals a thick braided necklace that matches a bracelet on his wrist, and an overwhelming presence of Brut cologne. He goes on, "I manage this real estate agency. If you find yourself fallin' in love with Ireland and plan to stay, let me know. I'll find ya' the perfect place at a grand price."

I croak out, "Nice to meet you."

"Well, your paperwork is all in order. A completed application and credit card on file for automatic debt of rent and deposit. Your deposit will be returned at the end of your stay, barring nothing is damaged at the cottage," John says smiling and nodding.

"Yes, Ms. Lynch explained everything to us when she sent the application," I reply.

Nonchalantly waving his hands, "I'm sure she did. Our Fionnuala is most efficient. Conscientious and thorough with everything she does. My best employee and never misses any an opportunity to do more."

I sneak a peek at Ms. Bland face, who appears unfazed by John's comments.

"I'll be gettin' ya the keys. I want to arrange a time next week to stop out and check on how ya and your wife are settlin'in. We'll have a proper visit or if ya want to look at other cottages to own, we can make that happen. Our village has seen an increase in the number of tourist passing through on day trips or staying in the village for a night or two." John heads into his office and returns with a ring of keys. He explains which key opens what.

I nod patiently and finally say, "Okay. Thank you for everything." Keys obtained, I climb back in the car, "Elvis is still in the building."

Karen's brows knit together, "Pardon?"

"I was talking to the gentleman who runs the office and he's apparently an Elvis fan."

"Young Elvis or old Elvis?"

"Closer to old with jet black pouf hair, side burns, and lots of gold jewelry."

"He sounds like a character. I'd like to meet him." Karen laughs.

"Oh, you will. He plans to set up a time to stop by the house and see how everything's going."

Karen smiles, "I can hardly wait."

We head to the cottage. Our rented home for the next three months is a single-story building, white stucco, red-shingled roof, shamrock green trim, and an array of small seedlings growing out of the gutters. The asphalt on the gently sloping driveway is cracked like the hard shell of an ice cream cone. The front and west side of the property are bordered with stone wall—tumbling heaps of fieldstone in all the colors of tan and grey. The front lawn has recently been cut and some pink flowers grow along the front of the house. Karen would know what they're called. She's been planting flowers for years, and I try not to decapitate them with the lawnmower.

Karen sighs, "I love it."

I have to duck to enter the front door, but Karen's shorter height has her dancing through the cottage.

Karen beams, "This place is wonderful. The kitchen and dining room have great natural light. The living room and bedrooms are cozy. There's even a separate laundry room with a washer and dryer. I have to admit I was worried that it wouldn't live up to what I saw in the pictures. I know this wasn't your first choice of where to stay, but I'm glad we're here."

"It's not that it wasn't my first choice. After years of training and practice, I'm always suspicious of things that appear too good to be true. I'm glad you're happy."

"But you like it, right? What was your first impression when you walked in?"

"The place is clean, and it looks like the furniture matches. If I remember to duck, I won't hit my head every time I leave or come back. The sofa might fit me. Or not."

"Really, that's the best you can do, 'The furniture matches.'"

"What? It does match."

Karen sighs and rolls her eyes, "What's that?" She points to a white vase of flowers on the kitchen counter. "Yellow carnations and daisies. They symbolize friendship and happiness. That is so thoughtful." Karen says.

I read the accompanying card out loud, "We're glad you have come to stay with us. Please accept the small gift that has been left in the refrigerator. --The Welcome Committee."

Karen opens the refrigerator and pulls out a wicker basket of food. "There's cheese, a loaf of homemade bread, crackers, strawberry preserves, coffee, milk, potatoes and a small ham, along with some chocolates. That is the nicest thing anyone could have done. Now we don't have to find the nearest grocery store yet tonight. We can just settle in. I'll try to find out who was so kind and thank them. It all makes me feel right about being here."

My stomach growls in agreement, "I'm sure someone at the reality agency will know who it is. When we go into town tomorrow, we can ask."

"Great. I'll start some dinner. How does ham and baked potatoes sound?"

"Sounds good to me, but can we start with cheese and crackers? I'm starving!"

Karen cuts slices of cheese, placing them along with the crackers on a plate. I make a pot of coffee. The aroma threading the air makes me feel relaxed and at home. Karen finishes a bottle of diet soda she picked up on the way to Ballyram. I'm missing beer, but I can survive one night. We munch on cheese and crackers. While her knife slices the ham, Karen asks, "What is the first thing you think we need to do tomorrow?"

"Find the closest pub!"

"Really, that's the biggest thing on your agenda?" Karen asks, snickering.

"Yep. My entire plan while here is to visit local pubs, do some sight-seeing, learn about this great culture, eat out in local pubs, take naps, read, and drink beer at local pubs. I have convinced myself that immersion in this culture is truly in my best interest, especially with a pint of beer in my hand."

Shaking her head, Karen laughs, "Good to know."

"While dinner is cooking, how about a short walk?" I ask.

As we step out the front door, twilight is turning the evergreen into shades of mute musk when we walk along the path that serves as a drain, walkway, bike path, and gutter. It's mostly flat and keeps the pedestrians as well as the drivers alert, since we have the stone walls to protect us and drivers have the stone walls to avoid. Karen takes my hand. Tiny stones click against our shoes, the Irish dirt feels like American soil, but smells boggy and clean. It's good to get the airline kinks out. Tomorrow the "Aventure" in our temporary hometown begins!

Chapter 2

It's nine in the morning on our first full day in town. I sit in a wooden lawn chair near the front door, enjoying my morning coffee. The sun is shining, it's a bit cool, and the smell of burning wood lingers in the air. All that's missing is the pint.

The front door opens, and Karen sticks her head out, "What are you doing?"

"Not much. I thought that was our plan."

"Good come back." Karen replies, "I was wondering about breakfast. I'd like to eat something light now and then go into town and look around. Lunch at the pub would be nice. We could start introducing ourselves to people in town. And we need to do some grocery shopping; the refrigerator is looking very empty."

"Good idea. We did eat nearly everything that we found in the 'Welcome' gift basket."

Our cottage is about a fifteen-minute walk from the heart of town on the pedestrian walkway, the car-defying path with slate walls on either side.

As we enter the village, Karen reads aloud the sign, "Ballyram. Population: 300." We complete one walk around town. The main street is lined with small shops in an array of colors. European rowhouse construction of several fronts butt up against each other.

Karen pauses, "Not what I expected, to see a bold canary yellow, mint green, tangerine, mixed in among the classic white with black trim and accents. I know I keep saying this, but I love it."

I'm happy Karen is happy. My stomach is not happy. My head tells my stomach that making Karen happy is more important than being full.

The main street, named Ballyram Street (go figure), is lined on two sides with shops including a coffee shop, grocer, bakery, the estate agent/insurance office, clothing stores, butcher shop, gift shop, a Chinese restaurant, a pub, and a betting shop. There are also several shops on the small second street, including another pub. This is a great tourist town. I'm staring down one of the secondary roads when Karen asks, "What are you looking at?"

"The police station. In Ireland, police are called the Garda."

"You would be the person to notice that." Karen snickers and pats my arm.

"Hey, I'm retired."

"I want you to be happy here, but please don't get too friendly with the local law enforcement. I know you miss being a detective, but this is our vacation."

"I promise. Can we go eat, please?"

We decide on the Lamb and Ram Pub. The pub is on the historical register and is over 200 years old. One of two pubs in the village, it sits in the middle of a block with the gift shop to its right and the betting shop to its left. The pub has a single wooden front door, stained with rain, and boasting a slight tinge of green. When we step inside, The Lamb and Ram feels warm inside. Rich brown wooden floors shine against the dark paneled walls. An aroma of wet wood, stale beer, and garlic hang in the room.

To our left is the bar and a third of the whole interior. It's a darker wood than the floors, but only slightly. Eight or nine stools sit in front of the bar. Stepping further into the room I see that the bar room extends further back. The conversation in the place has suddenly stopped and all eyes are upon us.

"I like it," I whisper to Karen. "I envision many a would-be writer, patriot, or statesman raising a glass in here." I say.

"Where do you want to sit?" Karen asks.

Five square tables form a row in line with the bar and an equal number of booths on the right. "The table to the far left."

"An easily defensible position?" Karen inquires smiling.

"Okay. Yes. Old habits die hard." I reply, laughing.

Karen sits with her back to the room, so that I have a visual on as much as possible.

Three men are sitting at the far end of the bar, and a couple snuggles in one of the booths. Patrons begin quiet conversations again.

"I'll buy two different lunches and we can decide who wants what later."

Karen laughs, "That works for me."

I make my way to the bar and my eyes catch the array of bottles against the back wall. The bartender questions, "Are you the Americans I've heard of?"

I pause to assess the bartender, early 30's with short, red tinged hair, and clear green eyes. "I'm not sure, kind of depends on what you heard," I reply.

"You're an American police detective. You and the missus rented Laird O'Connor's Baile Cottage up the way for three months."

"I'm surprised you know about us."

He shrugs without moving his shoulders. "In a village, most

people end up knowing your business for better or worse."

"Yes, we're renting the cottage, but I'm a *retired* American police detective. Dan Novice," I say, extending my hand, "and that's my wife, Karen." I point at Karen, who waves from the table.

He extends a large, tanned hand, calloused, with bitten nails that match the worry creases around his eyes. His hand shakes mine, then quickly drops to the bar where he fiddles with a ragged piece of paper napkin, "Welcome to Ballyram, I'm Brian Flynn, Owner and Proprietor of the Lamb and Ram. If you have any questions about the village, let me know. I was born and raised here as me father before me and his father before him. In case you didn't know, the local pub is the information center of all the village's news, gossip, advice and craic."

My head snaps back with a startle, "Crack?"

Brian laughs, "Yes, but not the one you're thinkin' of, Detective. This one is spelt C-r-a-i-c. It's Irish for "good fun."

Now it's my turn to laugh. "What's the difference between Gaelic and Irish?" I ask.

"Being born Irish," Brian replies, looking me straight in the eye. "To us, it's our language, Irish. Foreigners call it 'Gaelic.'"

I nod my head in understanding, "Well, thank you for the information. Pleased to meet you. We'd like to order lunch. What do you recommend?"

"The house specialty is Guinness and Beef Pie, and the Fish n' Chips is good. Me wife, Deidre, knows her way around the kitchen. I can assure you that you'll not be findin' a better Fish n' Chips for three counties." Brian's red hair moves with emphasis as his shoulders rise and fall once.

“I’ll take one Guinness and Beef Pie and a Fish and Chips. What beers do you have on tap?”

He brightens up, “I have a Fall’N Pumpkin, which is a seasonal beer, Smithwick’s, Murphy’s, Harp, and, of course, Guinness.

“I’ll need a Guinness now and another when lunch comes, also a diet cola for my wife.”

“Brilliant! An intelligent man knows what he likes. I’ll put that in straight away and bring it to the table when it’s ready.” I pick up my first pint of beer from the bar and carry it to the table, along with the diet soda. I’m struck by how smooth that first pint of dark ale is. If being in this pub with an Irish pint in my hand and Karen by my side is what hard work buys, it was worth every minute.

A young man approaches our table. He’s about 6’ tall, 185 pounds with sandy brown hair, clear blue eyes, and can’t be over 30 years old. He extends his hand, “I’m sorry to disturb you. I’m Peter Quinn, a sergeant with the local Garda. Just call me Quinn, everyone does.”

I repress a laugh. Law enforcement loves using only a last name. It’s how we answer the phone, and how others ask for us. I think of it as camaraderie. Apparently, it’s also the same in other counties.

I shake his hand, “I’m Dan Novice and this is my wife, Karen.”

Quinn leans close, “Pleased to meet you both. How are you enjoying being an Irish country squire?”

“I wouldn’t say I’m a squire, but I’ve nothing but praise for our welcome to the town and Ireland, itself.” I say taking another sip of my beer.

Karen points to an empty chair, "Please join us."

His smile fades into contemplation as he sits down, "Good to hear. I understand you're a retired police detective. How long were you a 'copper'?"

"How does everyone seem to know I'm a retired detective? We've been here a day."

"Village life. People pretty much know your business," Quinn replies.

"Well, I was in patrol for eighteen years and a detective for my last fourteen."

"What kind of detective were you?"

Laughingly I reply, "I'd like to think a good one."

Quinn snorts a laugh.

I continue, "If you mean did I specialize in something, the answer is no. The city where I worked wasn't large enough to need specialized detectives. There were about eight detectives, and we each did a little of everything. I normally handled fire investigation, computer crimes, crash investigations, evidence work, burglaries, and murder. Not that we had a great deal of murders. Larger cases might involve more than one detective and we would split up the job duties."

Quinn drops his shoulders and whispers, "I'm not meanin' to bother you while you're on holiday, but if you'd find some time to talk, I'd greatly appreciate it. I plan to sit for the Investigators exam in a few months and would like to run scenarios past a seasoned detective. Not much happens in Ballyram, except for speeding and the occasional drink driving."

Nodding my head and smiling, "I'd be happy to help in any way you think I can.

Quinn's shoulders relax and a smile creases his face. He shakes my hand enthusiastically, "Brilliant. I appreciate that. I'll call by your cottage in a day or two. Now I'll be leavin' you to enjoy your lunch. Nice to meet you both."

Karen and I reply in unison, "It was nice meeting you."

I add, "I look forward to talking with you."

I look at Karen, who's smiling and shaking her head.

"What?" I ask

"Nothing. Just you and young officers. I don't think there'll be a time when you wouldn't be willing to help."

Knitting my eyebrows together, "That's okay that I offered to meet him, isn't it?"

Karen pats my hand, "Yes, you're a great mentor. It's one of the things I love about you. However, we haven't been here twenty-four hours, and you're already getting cozy with the local police. He seems like a nice guy."

Karen changes the subject by pointing to a poster on the wall describing traditional Irish music every Friday night. She cheerfully says, "It would be fun to come out and support the local artists."

"I can think of nothing better, except supporting the local brewers while supporting the local artists." I agree.

"Being a beer connoisseur appears to be your favorite hobby." Karen laughs heartily.

The door opens, and we're treated to a whiff of Irish air from the front door of the pub. A woman, young enough to be our daughter, comes across the room toward us. "I thought I recognized you as you walked into to town. How are you settling in?"

"Are you . . .?" I ask.

"Fionnuala or 'Fi' for short. I'm the agent who leased the cottage to you." I can't help it, my detective assessments start working: Fi is a petite young lady about 22 years old, 5'3, 110 pounds with intense blue eyes and brown hair that falls right at her shoulder blades. During the correspondence with Fi over the past few months via phone and e-mail, I always found her polite and professional, but very driven.

Karen says, "As a first full day, so far, so good. The weather is beautiful and we're about to enjoy lunch in this fabulous pub."

Fi smiles, "Fabulous, huh?" Her eyes don't hold any humor. I tell my coppy sense to stop analyzing and take a vacation.

Fi leans into me, "I was thinking of you today. I'd like to invite you to the Autumn Festival we have at Baile Manor. Laird Arthur O'Connor does a social evening at his home and asked specifically if I'd invite you both. I know it's short notice, but the party is this Saturday. It's a wonderful event."

Laird O'Connor is also our landlord. I look at Karen and she gives me the "why not" look. It'd be a great way to get to know people in town. "That's very nice of him. Yes, we'll attend. Thank you," I say.

Fi exhales a sigh, pats my hand, and lets her fingers linger there, "Brilliant. I'll be getting you the particulars. I think you'll be enjoying yourselves."

"We look forward to it. Thank you for thinking of us," I say.

Karen adds, "I have a question: were you the person responsible for the gift basket of food we found in our refrigerator?"

Fi shakes her head, "No, I can't take responsibility for the idea. There are a couple of women in the village who act as a welcoming committee. Their names are Kathleen and Maeve. They're sisters, in fact. I'm glad you enjoyed their gesture."

"Please let them know it was a wonderful idea. We'd like their names and addresses to write a personal thank-you to each of them. It was so nice not to have to shop after arriving in town."

"I'll pass your message on and I'll be getting you their names and address." She gives Brian a wave as she passes him on her way out. Brian's eyes flame bright green: anger. I have seen the difference between anger and lust in people's eyes, and Brian's is definitely anger. Hot anger. I wonder what that's about. I turn to Karen and say, "That should prove interesting."

"I'm not exactly sure what's going on."

"What do you mean, 'going on'?"

Karen pauses, "I can't quite describe it. It's more a feeling, like there's something more here, but I can't be sure."

"Do you think she's in trouble of some kind?"

"No, I feel more like a chess game being played, but I don't know how or why. Maybe she's just trying too hard to have us feel welcome. When she was describing the party, she said, '*We* have at Baile Manor.' I'm wondering if she and the Laird have more than a working relationship. And what was with her comment about her the pub not being fabulous?"

"I guess we'll find out Saturday."

Early in our marriage, my wife would often report not liking someone for one reason or another. I was dismayed by her opinions with little to no evidence. Many times, we would be watching a murder mystery on television, and Karen would pick out the murderer early in the show because she didn't like the character. I'd debate with her, citing that you can't pick out a murder based solely on not liking the character. Karen would simply reply, "I'm sitting in my den, watching television, and I can if I want to." I've learned not to doubt my wife's "impressions" of people. The truth tends to reveal itself at some later point. Her sixth sense can be unnerving. She'd made a great detective.

Brian and his pint stop at the table, asking if he might join us. Apparently, he anticipated our answer, because he sits down, "I understand you're here for three months or so. Is that right?"

"Yes, it is," I reply.

"I hope you find life in the village enjoyable. If there is anything me wife or I can do to help you or make your stay more enjoyable, please ask. We have a small outside area in the back of the pub, and we have a few tables and chairs that sit on the bank of the river. I saw you talkin' with Fi Lynch. She was all aglow when you rented the place. She's a local realtor with big plans but little prospects. Word of caution to the wise: I'd be wary of that one if I were you."

My years on the job tell me to act slightly bewildered, "I don't know what you mean."

"I'm just letting you know to be careful with your secrets around her."

I'm about to ask for clarification on what that meant when Brian suddenly stands up and states, "I'll let you enjoy your lunch. Save room for dessert. Me wife makes the best Sticky Toffee Pudding." He leaves the table and walks behind the bar, his stride stiff.

I turn to Karen and mouth the words, "What's that?" Karen shrugs her shoulders and gives me the 'I'm not sure' look.

Brian returns a short time later with our food and dessert

menus. The Guinness and Beef Pie looks wonderful. My fish n' chips are the best I've ever had.

After several minutes Brian stops at the table, "How's your food?"

"It was truly wonderful. I know for myself I'll be ordering dessert," I say. Karen orders the Sticky Toffee Pudding with ice cream. I opt for the apple pie, ice cream and a cup of coffee.

When finished, I place the bill and money on the bar as we are leaving and say, "Thank you" to Brian.

Once outside Karen looks at me and says, "I need to walk."

Karen and I continue with a "To do" list. Doyle's Grocery is located about a block from the pub. Karen and I have a basic list that includes pretty much "one of everything." As we're checking out, Thomas Doyle, the owner, stops us and welcomes us to Ballyram. He's 5'9' 165 lbs. and 60-65 years old. He has thick white wavy hair on his head and in his ears. Deep brown eyes match his misaligned tie, fighting against lying flat on the well-worn tan shirt. He informs us that the store not only sells groceries, but rail passes as well as being the local post office.

"It was nice meeting you, Dan." Tom says.

Half way home, Karen shifts the bags, "We need to do a better job of metering out how much we buy each trip or get a small wagon. My arms are going to fall off."

"Yeah. Some cans are digging into my ribs and the bread keeps trying to escape."

It's at this point that we can look along the side road which leads to Baile Manor, home to Laird Arthur O'Connor. I catch glimpses of the manor house through the trees and bushes—pale stone, tall chimneys, the glare of sun on windows. I imagine the interior magnificent with tall ceilings, dark paneled rooms, and generations of family portraits on the walls. I find myself looking forward to the party.

The groceries put away, Karen decides to finish unpacking. I settle myself into the living room couch and start reading the local newspaper. Later, I realize I haven't seen Karen for a while. I walk into the bedroom and notice she's napping. I join her. An hour later we both wake up. Over dinner we discuss our plans for the next few days.

Karen looks up from the array of travel guidebooks, "The kids are coming for a visit in a few weeks and will want to see some of the sites."

"I know, but I'd be willing to see things more than once, if need be."

"Me too. Okay then, our first trip will be to Blarney Castle."

Chapter 3

Rolling onto my side I see Karen wide awake staring at me, "Wow, you're up early. You look like you're ready for the day. Is everything okay?"

Karen laughs, "Well, someone's snoring woke me."

"Oh sorry. The bed just felt so good."

"Well, I'm glad you're getting into this 'retirement thing' and having some down time. How about a light breakfast here and a walk into town? We can spend some time shopping or at least visiting stores we haven't been in. One that looked the most interesting was an apparel store."

I crane my neck to see the clock on Karen's side of the bed, "What time is it, anyway?"

"7 a.m."

"You want me to go clothes shopping? Okay, I bet I can find a cool local tee shirt."

"It's part of your new hometown. Think of it as investigating the local color."

If Karen knew how my coppy sense never retired, she'd never have used that phrase. But hey, if it makes her happy buying clothing, it's a fair trade for pub time.

Walking into the village, Karen gasps, "Look at that great old church at the top of the hill. Let's wander over to it. I think we can get to it if we turn left on this street here. The street sign says it's called Clover Road."

"What else would it be called in Ireland?" I say playfully.

St. Patrick's Catholic Church is constructed of grey block with a steep black roof, much of which is moss-covered; there's a single steeple. Next to the church is a cemetery, grey slate tombstones tilting from age, moss that looks as though it stopped, mid-slide along the headstones, small leaves covering the spaces between the stones. And the sense of quiet, eerily quiet.

"Kelly, 1789; Kennedy, 1803; Flynn, 1822," I read aloud.

Karen points, "This headstone is only four years old. How sad. This young man was only twenty-four years old when he died and it appears his sister was only nineteen." The stones are hard and too clean, too raw.

"I can't imagine losing one child, let alone two. Both so young. It was the part of the job I hated the most, having to tell a parent of their child's death." I shake my head, trying to free myself of the memories.

"Maybe we can see if a tour of the church and churchyard could be arranged. I'd love to know more of the history of my new hometown."

"That's a great idea."

From the church we look down onto Ballyram. It looks as if the buildings are arranged on a capitol cursive letter T.

Harvey's and Le Meilleure are on the corner where Ballyram and Clover meet. One side of the building is a men's clothing and the other is women's. 'Harvey's' is painted in wide gold letters on a dark green background while 'Le Meilleure' is depicted in flowery script with a lace border. It's like the men's boxer section romped into lingerie. Two front entrances stand about six feet apart, but apparently are one store. An uneasy alliance? The union of two nationalities? Or simply a way to combine two attitudes into one store? Karen and I enter on our respective sides.

A small, round gentleman greets me, "I'm Harvey Clarke, Proprietor, of *this* side. My wife oversees the other half. Is there something special you're looking for?"

"I'm Dan Novice and that's my wife, Karen. We're new in town and getting familiar with the village."

"My store has fine Irish wool suits, quality dress and casual shirts, as well as most men's clothing items and accessories. I also have an on-site tailor for any item, if needed."

I look over to see a tall, rail thin woman approach Karen. The woman's hair is not naturally blond. I move closer to the women's side and listen to the woman speak to Karen: "This store is a reflection of my vision to bring French culture and fashion to Ballyram. *La Meilleure* means 'The Best' in French. I'm from here but studied design in Paris. I'm Claire." As Claire speaks, I join Karen and am mildly entertained watching Claire swings her arms out in front of her as she speaks French. Karen and I stand there with blank looks on our faces.

"I'm sorry; when I'm excited, French just pops out of my mouth without my thinking about it. Any time you need something to wear for a special event, please stop here first. My inventory is very selective, and many are one of a kind. I'd be embarrassed to see two of my clients at the same event wearing the same outfit." Claire leans into Karen, whispering, "Also I rarely carry any design in a size larger than a 10. I'm sure you're aware that French fashion is not for our "big girls," if you know what I mean." Claire winks.

Karen nods politely. Harvey makes a sound that could be a

snort. Claire feels a bit too pretentious for a small village. Chalk up another couple for 'interesting marriages in the Ballyram.'

Claire coos, "I'm guessing you're the Americans that the village is talking about. Am I right?"

I have a snide remark ready on my lips but squash my American sarcasm.

"Yes. I'm Karen Novice and this is my husband, Dan. It's nice to meet you both."

"Welcome to Ballyram. I understand both of you have been invited to Laird O'Connor's event." Claire points to Karen, "I have the perfect outfit for you! It just arrived yesterday."

We must have quizzical looks on our faces because Claire replies, "Small village. Secrets are poorly kept, unless one of the people is dead." Claire cackles as she moves to a rack near the back of the store, "It's a calf length, black crepe dress with a matching jacket the same length as the dress. You're a size 6 in the U.S., correct?"

"Yes," Karen replies.

"I insist you try it on." Claire escorts Karen to the dressing room. I notice Karen is not objecting.

Harvey looks at the clothing, humming to himself while he rearranges ties on a rack. I watch him, Claire, and the dressing room curtain. When Karen steps out of the dressing room, I decide the new dress looks amazing.

"Magnifique! It was made for you, my dear," Claire exclaims.

Karen's mouth quirks. "I'm not sure. Wouldn't this be a bit too dressy?"

"Laird O'Connor's event is *the* event of the season. It's the finest catering, the best linens, live music, the Laird's Waterford collection on display," Claire pauses, as though we are expected to understand, then continues, "Laird O'Connor and his family have been the caretakers, benefactors, and symbol of class in the village for centuries. His presence gives continuity in the village's very existence."

As Claire speaks, I wonder why we're invited. We don't know the Laird. We aren't of nobility nor the "upper crust."

As if he was reading my mind, Harvey states, "Laird O'Connor is most interested in talking to you, Dan. His Lairdship fancies himself in the vein of Sherlock Holmes. He thought it'd be fun speaking with an American police detective. The Laird has remarked on several occasions that he can identify a murderer in a book before the fourth chapter. Come prepared to discuss your most baffling case. The greater the intrigue the better."

"What had you planned on wearing, if not my beautiful suggestion?" Claire's eyebrows ripple below her frown. Her voice has a hint of petulance.

"Um. Something warm, like wool pants, a silk blouse and a wool blazer." Karen replies.

Claire shakes her head emphatically, "Pah! My dear that simply will not do! I see an attention to detail and quality in the clothes you're wearing. I know you're not someone who considers a set of Wellies an accessory. Truly, you have a discerning eye. I insist you buy the dress, but if you decide you don't like it, please bring it back, and I'll personally shop my store to find something perfect for you. What do you say?"

Karen looks at herself in the mirror and gasps, "This dress does look like it was made for me and this fabric feels amazing. I'll take it."

Harvey turns to me, I tell him before he can ask, "I have a pair of quality dress pants, white French cuff shirt with a set of cuff links my wife bought me, and a tie." That appears to satisfy him. Harvey's not the power salesperson in the couple.

Karen and I leave fifteen minutes later with her purchase in hand. After two blocks she says, "I wasn't planning on that, but I might've been underdressed with what I was planning to wear."

"I'm positive you'll look beautiful." Walking past the bait store reminds me that I wanted to try some fishing or 'angling,' as the locals call it. I turn to Karen, "I'm going to check out this store. Do you want to come with me or should we meet somewhere?"

"I'm more fashion, less fishing. I'd like to go into the gift store next to the Lamb and Ram. I'll meet you there in twenty minutes. Okay?"

Twenty minutes later I see Karen standing outside of the gift shop and she looks as though she's dying to tell me something.

"What's up?"

"I met our Welcome Basket ladies, Maeve and Kathleen. I was looking around the store to see if anything would make nice gifts to take back to the U.S. or for when people visit here. You know how Hannah talked about wanting a fairy garden."

The thought of our five-year-old granddaughter brings a smile to my face.

Karen continues, "Maeve Kelly's about 60-65 years old and as round as she is tall. Has stick straight white hair that's cut very short and buzzed on the sides. She introduced her sister, Kathleen, who's her opposite. She's maybe a few years younger, but skinny as a bean pole and just as tall as Maeve. Her hair is long and sort of just droops from her head. She seemed quiet until she talked about the collection of fairy statues in the store, then she lit up."

"And?" I ask.

"When I first came in the store there was one other person there. She was a young woman, maybe 30ish, about my height, heavier, with dark blond hair, but with the most striking blue eyes I've ever seen. It looked like she was picking up a package in the shop. After the girl left, I didn't mean to eavesdrop, but they weren't whispering either. The one who turned out to be Maeve, said, 'Isn't just terrible her husband is the way he is. She must be a saint to have gone back to him and him not changing any.'" Karen pulls me closer and continues, "Kathleen said that 'she prays for the dear every Sunday' and went on to say that 'he has always been selfish, even as a boy.' Maeve laughed and said, 'I'm sure he's not so high and mighty with his drinking and carousing, knowing that his Lairdship is more than willing to help meet her needs.' Then they both laughed. I shouldn't have listened, but it was impossible not to. I get the feeling this village is more Peyton Place, less Mayberry."

I'm intrigued, "Who do you think the girl was?"

"I have no clue, but her husband must be a gem," Karen replies sarcastically.

"Do you think they were referring to Laird O'Connor?"

"I don't know if there is more than one 'Lairdship' in town."

"Anything else?"

"I wandered to the back of the store, so it wouldn't look like I was listening. When I went to check out, the woman behind the counter introduced herself. They knew who I was. Maeve started talking to me and informed me that she runs the gift shop while her sister cares for their bed and breakfast, but they help each other out. They both still live in their childhood home, which is now the Captain's Bed and Breakfast. I'm invited for tea tomorrow."

"That was very nice of them to invite you over."

"I don't think I had a choice. Maeve is a force of nature. The invitation sounded more like an expectation than an invitation."

"That sounds like it should be interesting," I laugh.

"I'm sure I'll know more about this village than I need to before the end of tea tomorrow. How about we take a slow walk around town before heading home?"

"Sure." I reply, "Anywhere in particular you would like to walk?"

"I'd like to see if the Chinese and Indian restaurants have their menus posted outside. We may want something to eat besides pub food. First let's look at the bakery."

"Good idea."

Our next stop is at the bakery. I open the door, and it makes a slight whooshing sound combined with the tingle of an overhead bell. I step into the warm air that smells of fresh bread, vanilla, and peanut butter.

Karen asks, "You okay? You look as if you're a million miles away."

"I just had a flashback. Every Sunday, my grandfather and I would attend 8:30 a.m. Catholic Mass. My stomach often growled in church and on the way home; we would stop at a small family owned bakery for a 'snack.'"

A low din of voices filters from the back room; then a middle-aged gentleman appears and asks if we need help. I introduce Karen and myself.

"I'm the owner, Tim Clarke."

"Are you any relation to Harvey Clarke of Harvey's Mens Store."

"I am. Harvey and I are brothers. Harvey being the older of us." Once the connection is made, the family resemblance is unmistakable. The facial and body shapes are the same, but the most compelling feature is their blue eyes, which are a complete duplicate of each other.

I compliment him on his wares. He beams with pride and appears to enjoy them by the look of his weight. The last button on his plaid flannel shirt, the one that rests just above his belt is in jeopardy of popping.

Plain, chocolate-filled, vanilla-covered, and sprinkled donuts. Rye, wheat, white, long, round, sliced, whole, plain, sesame-covered breads, and more fill the cases. We have to control ourselves from buying one of everything. Karen and I discuss our options and we end up buying a loaf of brown bread and a loaf of soda bread. We thank Tim and make our way out.

Karen and I continue walking around town. The sun is shining on us and all I can think is that I'm happy. I buy Karen a dozen red roses from a cart outside the grocery store.

"Red roses symbolize love, correct?" I ask.

Karen buries her nose in the bouquet then smiles up at me, "Yes. Yes, they do."

I have the love of my life with me and we're both healthy enough to enjoy what we've earned. As I'm lost in thought, the sound of raised voices gains my attention.

"Aye, I'm up for a ruck anytime. You'll be sorry, ya dam eejit. You should be dead. Get on with ya."

I swivel my head to determine where the argument is coming from and who is involved when I get body checked from Brian Flynn coming out of Clarke's Bakery.

"Whoa!" I take a step back.

Brian mutters under his breath, "Sorry," but he doesn't stop or make eye contact. I look at Karen, then at Tim standing in the doorway, red faced enough to explode. Before I can ask him a question, he turns and steps back into the store.

Karen looks at me bewildered, "What was that about?"

"I don't know but it's not good. What do you think a 'ruck' is?"

"I have no clue. Fight? Maybe it's a bad word in Irish." Karen shrugs her shoulders, "What's an eejit?"

"My first thought is 'idiot.'"

Karen and I finish our walk about the village and stroll home. As we leave the village, Karen turns to me and whispers, "I think there are a lot of secrets behind these doors. The village appears quaint, but I sense something here. I hope they're just petty neighbor squabbles, but I can't shake the feeling they aren't."

Chapter 4

Karen and I make our way into the village for a quick shopping trip. Karen grabs a basket and head for the produce aisle. I make my way to the frozen foods, specifically ice cream. Next to the freezer is a curtain covering the doorway to the back of the store. I hear low voices coming from behind the curtain.

"It doesn't matter. He'll be gone soon. Just be patient," says a male voice. A second voice, I can't tell if it's male or female, replies, "It does matter. He knows things. Things that can hurt everything we have planned. He has to be stopped any way we can." My curiosity piqued, I move closer to the curtain. I think I smell a hint of Brut cologne.

"Don't be an eejit. Calm down. He doesn't know anything. He *thinks* he knows something. He's not a threat if we keep our heads. Now go back to work and stop your drinkin.'"

"Get off me drinkin'. It's not a problem. You're the problem. Stop taunting him. What if he goes to the Garda?" The second person hisses.

"Let him go to the Garda. He's got nothin' I tell ya. All he's got is a story. Nothin' worth believin'. Besides who's gonna do anything? Foley? He's dumber than dirt and the new wonder boy isn't any better," the man snaps.

I still can't place the voices.

"He can ruin everything. What about the American?" The

second voice rises to a panicky pitch.

"Pah, forget the American. He's not one of us. We keep him out of village business and then everything will go the way we want." Suddenly I hear a door close from behind the curtain. Someone went out a back door. I attempt to hurry toward the front door. I see someone in a deep crimson colored shirt exiting out of the store. It may have been John Shea. Then I hear, "Ah, Dan, good to see you again. Anything in particular you're lookin' for?" I turn and am face to face with Tom Doyle, store owner. Is it my imagination or is his face a bit flush? Where did he come from? Was he one of the men in the back room?

"Ahh . . . no. Karen and I just stopped in for a few things. I was about to have a look at the ice cream. Thank you."

Tom nods affirmatively and wanders toward the front of the store. I grab a carton of ice cream and join Karen.

"I thought you hated strawberry ice cream." Karen says.

"Uhh?" Looking at the basket, I realize I grabbed the wrong flavor, "I guess I wasn't paying attention. I'll put it back and get vanilla."

"Are you okay? You seem distracted." Karen asks. Tom is again nearby, and I wave off Karen's concern. I return the ice cream and pick up the right one. Karen and I check out and when leaving, I say to Tom, "Enjoy your day."

When we arrive home, I explain to Karen what I heard.

"Who do you think was talking?" She asks.

"I don't know. The voices weren't loud enough to be able to distinguish who was speaking. I'm curious who they were referring to when they mentioned 'the American'? It could be us. Or are there other Americans living in the village?"

“Or Mr. X.”

“Mr. X? What’s that mean?” Cocking my head to understand her train of thought.

“The unknown factor. Someone we know nothing about.”

“Hopefully it’s nothing menacing. I guess we’ll just have to be extra vigilant.”

Karen raises her eyebrows at me and my coppy senses. Then she reminds me that she will be gone in the afternoon. My plans for the day include a nap, reading, and eating anything I can find in the house. Karen leaves at 11 a.m. and I settle in with leftovers and my book. A nap takes an hour of my time.

Once home, Karen is excited to tell me about her day. “The sisters run the town’s oldest bed and breakfast at the outer edge of the town. Their home faces the river and it’s beautiful. A classic white house with black trim around each window, and the front door is black too. They gave me a tour of all three floors. The first floor is where the sisters and their father each have a bedroom, a private sitting room, and the dining room where they serve breakfast for their guests. The dining room has a set of French doors that open onto a small patio and an immaculate garden.”

“It sounds nice.”

“I figure some of our guests could stay there if they don’t want to stay with us when they visit,” she says. I listen intently. People not staying with us 24/7 could be a good thing. Karen continues, “The sisters are a wealth of knowledge regarding the town, its history, and gossip. Kathleen is the town librarian and Maeve is head of the Ballyram Historical Society.

“Really.”

Karen appears very pleased with herself and says, “Yes and

they would love to give us a walking tour of the town and its history. I've learned that being the "American" in town has its advantages. They asked a few questions about me but were more interested in gossiping about the town. I encouraged them with appropriate ooohs and aahhs and an occasional gasp. I learned a few interesting tidbits. First, Laird O'Connor is a reported player especially with younger women both here in town and some other cities, including Dublin where he met a woman named Colleen Moore."

"Did they say with whom here in town?" I ask, thinking about Fi inviting us to the Laird's party as though it were her party too.

"They wouldn't go as far as naming names. They did mention that there has been a cloud hanging over the Laird since his wife died. She had terminal cancer, and the night of her death it appeared that she might have had some help with her passing. Kathleen said that Lady O'Connor was truly beloved. Her death was investigated, but because of the Laird's position, they think the city officials let him off by ruling it 'natural causes.'"

"Meeting our host will be interesting, knowing that information." I say, though my coppy senses are starting a profile of Laird O'Connor. I wonder if it will match the man I meet.

"Second, Maeve and Kathleen said that Colleen Moore made her fortune because she owned a software company and sold her stock two months prior to a hostile takeover. Maeve said that there is some kind of an investigation into Ms. Moore, possibly insider information. They speculate she's working on 'retiring to a quiet country estate.' Also, apparently the Laird is tight for cash and Ms. Moore is working on an arrangement with him," she pauses and raises her eyebrows, "in the form of marriage. Ms.

Moore buys her title and country estate, and the Laird would be able to keep hold of the family home."

"Trying to buy respectability, huh? I wonder what the locals think of that? Did Maeve say anything more about that?"

"No. However, my understanding is that Laird O'Connor and his first wife had one son, Michael, who has been estranged. Apparently, he'd been a problem child for many years."

I think about the family fights and domestic disturbances in my career. Some of the ugliest calls.

"Apparently Michael didn't even come back for his mother's funeral. Maeve heard Michael is living on the streets of Dublin as a vagrant."

A long-lost heir, now that's interesting. Did the ladies say anything else?"

"They were interested in our dealings with Fionnuala Lynch. They asked several times if we paid Fi directly for finding us the cottage or the real estate company. Maeve commented that Fi has expensive tastes and positive cash flow, but they know for sure her job doesn't pay well and wonders where Fi's money comes from. They were happy to hear we paid the office and not Fi directly. I think there's a story there."

"Huh. I wonder what their interest in Fi is?"

"Maeve and Kathleen go for coffee each Thursday morning after the village's Beautification Committee Meeting. They asked me to join the committee, even if it's temporary. I think I might just do that. I'd like to meet some of the other villagers."

"Anyone we know on the committee?" I ask.

"Maeve, Kathleen, Tim from the bakery, and some others. It might be fun to be part of."

"And pick up the gossip? It certainly would give you something to do, if you're interested." My thoughts go back to Fi's clothes and jewelry. Are they expensive or do they just look that way?

"Oh, the other interesting thing is Kathleen believes in fairies."

"Fairies, like the little flying girls of legend?"

"Yes. We started talking about the history of Ireland with its legends and myths. That's when Kathleen corrected me and said that fairies are real, and she had had contact with some."

The look on my face must have shown my skepticism.

"I know it sounds crazy, but Kathleen didn't make it sound crazy. Apparently, the fairies in Ireland are called 'sidhe' which was pronounced like shee and live in something called a 'rath,' but Kathleen made the word sound like 'rahs.' I may be mispronouncing the word. Anyway, Kathleen said the fairies' homes often look like ordinary piles of rocks. To move or get rid of them brings bad luck."

My curiosity is piqued. I lean forward and say, "Where does Kathleen go to meet her fairies?"

"She wouldn't say exactly. All she'd say is that it's quiet and people rarely go there. I got the feeling it's fairly remote, but I'm not sure."

"That's different." I lean back, intrigued.

"The way Kathleen explains it, I almost believe her. She seems gentle and kind. I'm positive she believes it. She talked about each fairy as an individual with a personality. Apparently, fairies love music and dancing. Fairies can make themselves known to humans by appearing to them. If the fairies contact a human, then you can hear their music and see them dancing. She also said there are evil fairies, and humans need to be wary of them and not follow them into the woods. I think Hannah would be fascinated to speak with Kathleen when she's here for a visit."

I bristle at introducing my granddaughter to an adult who believes in fairies, "Hannah is only five years old. I'm not sure it's wise to introduce her."

Karen rolls her eyes, "Don't worry. Kathleen isn't dangerous. She's a very sensitive individual and this is very much a part of her culture. Hannah will love the idea of fairies and their world. I'll spend more time with Kathleen and Maeve before Hannah arrives to be sure they're good people."

"Okay, okay. You know I have a hard time believing in such things."

"I know, I know. You spent a lifetime writing up reports of what happened, not what you *think* happened. Kathleen did say something strange. She said something about how someone in the village is trying to hurt where the fairies live, and that person will be sorry if he goes ahead with the plan."

"What do you think she meant?" I sit forward in my chair.

"I don't know. She said, 'He can't just do that. He should know the rules.' Maeve jumped in and told her 'to stop goin' on with that silliness.' Kathleen snapped that it wasn't silliness and 'we just have to wait and see.'"

"Kathleen sounds serious. I'd be curious to find out more about what she was talking about. I'll leave that up to my capable partner, if you will."

"Okay, I'll do my research before Hannah arrives. Change of subject, how about a walk before dinner?"

We walk down the lane, and pass what we've come to call "the farmer's field," as though there's only one farmer in Ireland. It's a storybook one, with random outcrops of round stones, and the dun-white colors of sheep, their teeth mowing the land, their hooves moving quietly along the pasture grass. They ignore us, continue grazing, and sometimes switch their wooly brushes of a tail. Sheep are quiet, or quieter than I thought. I enjoy watching them, and then I notice two black and white Border collies lying in the field, heads lifted toward us, with a careful eye on their wooly wards. I'm lost in thought when I hear an angry voice with a heavy Irish brogue, "Aye, what are ya doin' there?"

I realize it's the sheep farmer. He's is standing partially down his driveway and waving a walking stick.

Startled, I respond, "Just watching the sheep."

"Well, boyo, they're not pets. Leave them alone. And they aren't for sale. You one of the surveyor guys snooping round for the grand man? Well, you're not gettin' me land. Be off with ya before I turn me dogs on ya!"

So much for peaceful farmland. Karen turns back toward the road and quickens her steps. I back away from the fence with my hands up and reply, "Sorry. Not interested in buying anything. I'm not some surveyor guy. I'm just your neighbor and on vacation. I meant no harm. Again, I'm sorry if we bothered you."

"I'm not believin' ya. Get away with yourself. This is still my land." The farmer maintains his position on his driveway.

Karen and I don't feel like walking farther; silently we turn from the far side of the road and walk home.

"That is one angry man," I state.

"Yeah! I had just been thinking that Hannah would like to see the sheep up close when she's here, but I don't think we'll ask the 'Angry Farmer.'"

"I'm curious what he meant with the comments of the 'grand man' and 'you're not getting my land.'"

Karen shakes her head, "My first thought about the grand man would be Laird O'Connor, but why would he want that guy's land?"

"Basic neighbor dispute. Maybe it's about the property line or about something like disagreeing over who owns a tree. I ran into that a lot. Neighbors complaining that the other person blew leaves or grass or whatever onto their lawn."

"But this is Ireland? Wouldn't people have worked that out a long time ago? What new project would get people so angry?" Karen sighs, "I guess we won't stop by his farm again."

"Now what do you want to do for excitement?"

"I've had enough excitement for one day. Thanks," Karen laughs. "But speaking of Hannah, I plan to video conference with her tomorrow morning. I hope I calculated the time difference correctly."

Back at the cottage we have dinner after which we settle in with our books and later call it a night. I keep playing the encounter with the farmer over and over in my head. My professional curiosity may require I learn more about the back story on the farmer.

Chapter 5

For our first 'aventure,' Karen wants to see the legendary Blarney Castle. The day dawns bright and clear, a bit cool. We layer in jeans, tee shirts and flannels, and toss windbreakers, or as the Irish say, 'wind cheaters,' into the car before setting off.

"I wonder how one says, 'road trip' in Irish.?" Karen laughs

We start out on the road as the sun is peeking through the trees and shining down on the rolling hills. It feels right to be here. Clear skies and signs printed in English help boost my confidence driving to an unfamiliar area in a foreign country on narrow roads. I'm still amazed by this country. The rolling hills of sun and shadows, pastures, slate walls, farm buildings and houses set back from the road, and exquisite manor houses fill my view. A few hours of driving melt away quickly.

I find a parking spot on the street and figure out the parking meter system. It's still early and the castle is closed, so we find a restaurant. Inside there's a lunch counter with half a dozen stools to the left hand side and eight or nine square metal tables with Formica tops and matching chairs scattered to the right. Karen and I are met with a mixture of voices, the smell of hot oil, coffee, and sweet aroma of pancakes.

A woman, approximately 45 years old, brown hair pulled back with a thick rubber band, and wearing her blue and white checked uniform, yells from behind the counter, "Seat where you like, and I'll bring you some menus straight away."

I maneuver Karen toward a table for two near the back of the restaurant. Even before we sit down, the hostess approaches with menus saying, "Your waitress will be with you soon. Coffee this morning?" Karen and I affirm that question.

This morning I relish the first sips of the black nectar and feel comfort. Now I can focus on the menu. The item that catches my eye is the buttermilk pancakes served with orange-honey butter and maple syrup.

Our waitress appears from the kitchen. I make eye contact with her and she drops a plate of toast she's carrying. All the color drains from her face. She hurries to throw the toast in the garbage and proceeds to approach our table. Her name tag says 'Nora.'

"Are you alright?" Karen asks.

Nora nods, but is still noticeably shaking. She squeaks out, "What can I get ya?"

Karen and I order. Nora turns, practically running into the kitchen.

"Was it something we said?" I ask Karen.

"She looked absolutely terrified before she even began talking to us. Is there someone here she's afraid of?"

I begin to survey the room, "No, don't see anything. So, I don't know what's scaring our waitress."

Nora arrives with our breakfasts. Nora shakily refills our coffee cups and asks if there is anything else she can bring. We both say no.

We settle in with our breakfasts and are lost in the joy of eating. I pay the cashier and head back to the table. I hear Karen ask Nora if she is alright.

Nora whispers, "I'll be knowin' this to be strange, but I'm a 'sensitive.'"

"I'm not sure what you mean," Karen states.

"Since I was a wee child I saw things others couldn't."

Karen places a hand on Nora's arm, "Like what?"

"I see dark shadows around you and your husband. The Costa Bower will come soon."

Karen steps back, "What's a Costa Bower? What does that mean?"

"The death coach that carries away the spirit of the dead. Someone near you will die soon."

"What? Who? What are you saying?"

"Be aware and stay safe." Nora turns and flees into the kitchen.

Karen shakes her head and sighs, "Apparently there is a Specter of Death hanging around us."

"Well, he's paying for his own ticket for the castle tour," I laugh.

Karen's voice takes on a serious tone, "I think she truly believed it. And to tell you the truth, so do I. I feel like something bad is going to happen."

"Hey, I don't believe in those things, so let's forget it and enjoy our day." I say, though I want to shake this off as a joke, but I can't. Karen's 'feelings' tend to be more right than wrong.

Karen nods, "But it still creeped me out." I hug Karen. I don't know what else to say.

The weather has turned gray and it has begun to drizzle. Luckily, we packed our waterproof jackets and pants. Karen and I enter the small building at the entrance of the grounds and pay our fee. The rain has discouraged some tourists. We begin our walk to the base of the castle. The paved walkway is glazed over as it meanders through a park-like setting with green lawns and mature trees. We approach the castle that was built in 1446. It is a mighty, imposing fortress, tall enough that we tip our heads backward to look at its height, dark grey in the rain. Heavy. It looks heavy with history. It also looks lonely. No one has lived in it since it does not have basic amenities such as heat, running water, or for that matter a roof. Three stories high, grey stone. We follow the worn, wooden arrows that direct us to the Blarney Stone. A cement sidewalk winds around the outer wall to entrance. The girth of the walls is evident as we enter the first room. No ducking required. At the end of the lower level are the stairs. The castle stairways are narrow, definitely one-person wide, made of stone, and a little slippery due to the drizzle. Slow and steady is best for my footing and for my knees. The stone walls are cold and worn from years of being touched by the elements, visitors, and history. The climb is not for those afraid of heights. Although there are walls, there is no glass in the windows and the view reinforces the distance between myself and the ground below.

Karen says, "Should we head to the very top of the castle because that's where we kiss the Blarney Stone? Then on the way down we can 'investigate' the other parts of the castle."

"Sounds like a plan to me." Only several dozen more stairs to go.

"Wow, the view!" Karen says it all.

We are at the top of the castle, drizzly skies above us and grey stone under our feet. I can see for miles in all directions. Karen and I stop to look around. It's a postcard of the Irish countryside: green fields roll softly downhill, stone walls create an irregular grid, and sheep appear placed by design for us 'out-of-towners.' Karen tugs my sleeve. We move toward a gentleman sitting on a mat with his legs hanging off a ledge at the far end of the roof dangling above the rebar safety net. He looks up, "Come here, Love" and pats a mat on the floor next to him.

Tourists unafraid of heights or eager to increase their BS potential, lie on their back on top of the mat, reach back to grasp a metal handle on each side of their head that is secured to the outer wall, lean back, and with help from the gentleman, are slid forward in a partial back bend until their lips touch the stone with the instruction, "Kiss," and then are helped to back.

"Ladies first," I tell Karen.

"Oh, so I have a few minutes' advantage on you. Or so you can watch if I get frightened of heights?"

The solemn gentleman with the safety net speaks up, "Nobody gets afraid, me girl. We are here to care for you."

"We?"

"All of us. The spirits of the castle, the spirits of Ireland, and Irish thought. And me."

I want to do an eye roll, but Karen is listening. She settles herself on the mat, lies on her back, scoots backward until she can grip the safety bars. Then the gentleman leans to help as her head tilts toward the stone, kiss, and it's finished. She's back standing on the stone pavement.

I take Karen's picture and she takes mine. Not that anyone would have trouble believing my innate talent for spinning the words. When done, we admire the view of the surrounding area. Karen and I continue to explore the various rooms in the castle on our way down to ground level.

Finding a restroom in an Irish castle requires a bit of detective work. I join Karen as she strolls the castle grounds. Her face is alight with eagerness, "I was just talking to the most interesting man." Karen swivels her head in all directions, "Where did he go? He was here just a minute or so ago. They must have actors playing parts. He said that we 'should see the gardens in the spring, they're a sight to behold, colors as bright as the sun!' He went on to tell me where the legend of the "gift of Blarney" comes from. That's so odd, he couldn't have gone that far that fast."

"Well, tell me what he said."

"The legend goes that it comes from Lord of Blarney, Cormac McCarthy, who owned the castle and land in the late 1580s. He didn't want to give his land to Queen Elizabeth as she expected all Irish landowners to do under England rule. The Lord would write crafty letters to the Queen, full of flattery and proclaiming his loyalty to the Crown, with no intention of giving his land to the Queen. After receiving one of the Lord's letters, it is said that the Queen stated, 'This is all blarney.' Hence a legend was born. Now anyone who kisses the stone is said to be bestowed with eloquence or the gift of gab."

"That's interesting."

"So 'blarney' is used to mean anyone speaking with eloquence or exaggerating but turning an empty phrase. But what was really funny is he said that Ireland is full of things man cannot explain. Then he said something odd, "The woman with shoulders of white holds the key."

"What do you think he meant by that?"

"I don't know. That's when I turned to see if you were coming. When I looked back, he was gone."

"That's weird. Where to next?" I ask.

"I'd like to visit a few of the gardens on the grounds. I'm especially interested in the Poison Garden," Karen says.

My head snaps up and I look at Karen, "You're interested in the Poison Garden, why?"

"Because in the medieval era, they were called Physic Gardens and the plants were used for medical reasons."

"Now they're called Poison Gardens?"

Karen states, "Many of our early medicines and even some today come from poisonous plans." She giggles, "I think it's interesting and I may need to get rid of you some day."

I laugh too. Arriving at the garden, I see signs clearly indicating that the plants are poisonous and are not to be touched or eaten. Most are in cages.

"There's one I'm very familiar with. Cannabis Stiva," I say pointing to a large cage.

Karen shakes her head, "Yes, the cop would notice the marijuana plant."

I'm surprised by the number of plants and their uses. "I didn't know that rhubarb leaves are poisonous. I love rhubarb pie."

"You like most kinds of pie." Karen smirks, "The stalks are fine for pie. The leaves were an early laxative."

We stop at various plants, I say, "Rican Communis or Rican and Deadly Nightshade. They're still in the news and not in a good way."

"True, but we eat others forms of nightshade, such as tomatoes, eggplant and even potatoes." Karen points to a small plant, "Foxglove is digitalis that is still used to treat heart conditions."

Karen and I follow slate-laid paths through a few other

gardens. It begins to rain harder. We can see the castle, grey and damp-looking, blending in to the grey cloudy sky.

Karen shivers, "It looks as if the rain isn't going to stop any time soon. Are you ready to leave? Everything is overcast and cold and it's going right through me."

Once home Karen heads off to take a hot bath. We decide on dinner in Ballyram. Opening the door to the Lamb and Ram, I feel as if I uncorked a bottle: sounds of talking, laughing, and glasses clinking. The air in the room is warm and thick with wonderful smells of hot oil and fish.

Brian shows Karen and me to a table for two at the back of the room, "I'm glad to see ya again."

"We enjoy it here, and we're interested in the live band tonight."

Brian appears to swell with pride, but I'm wondering if it's coincidence that he's wearing the same shirt I saw him wearing the first time we were here. Small wardrobe? Keep the same things for the pub? Lack of time? Or trouble with the wife? I tell my coppy sense to take a break.

I go to the bar to order. I return with a pint of Guinness and a diet cola for Karen.

Karen covers her mouth with her hand and leans into me, "Who's the girl behind the bar?"

"That's Deidre, Brian's wife. He introduced me to her when I placed our order."

"*That's* the girl in the lace shop that Maeve and Kathleen were talking about," Karen whispers.

"Brian is the guy the sisters were talking about drinking and stepping out on his wife?"

"That would mean she's the girl that Laird O'Connor is interested in."

Leaning back in my chair, I sneak a glance at Brian, "As Alice said about Wonderland, "Curiouser and curiouser."

"Do you think it's true?"

"I have no idea." I answer. Several minutes later Brian brings our dinners to the table.

Karen savors her first bite of Shepard's Pie. "Perfect. It's a bowl of comfort food."

"Good to hear. My Fish N'Chips is great and I have the perfect condiment to it all, beer! Karen rolls her eyes.

I notice that Brian is making his way around the room, stopping at nearly every table, a pint in his hand.

As Brian moves back behind the bar, Tom Doyle, from the grocery store, stops at our table, "How are ya likin' your time in the village?"

Karen replies, "We love it! People have been very welcoming."

"Brilliant. It's rare havin' new people who stay here. We have tourists during the summer. It's good to see ya in the pub. Me daughter Diedre and her husband own it. I been hearin' you're a retired detective. Is it true?"

"I was in law enforcement for over thirty years."

"That's a long time. You earned yourself a rest. Well, not much happens here except the occasional drunken argument, but soon all is forgiven, and life goes on." Tom shrugs his shoulders, "Usually."

I knit my eyebrows together, as I don't know what to make of his statement, but before I can ask, Tom says, "Well, the people of the village are glad you're both here. Me youngest daughter,

Molly, is in the band tonight. She plays the bodhran, and her cousin, Kathryn, plays the flute."

Karen tilts her hear to one side, "The bodhran?"

Smiling, Mr. Doyle replies, "The bodhran is a traditional hand held Irish drum. The other members of the band are Patrick who is the guitarist and lead singer, Matthew who plays the fiddle, and Paddy who plays the concertina."

"A concertina is a small accordion, right?" I say.

"Right you are. Well, I'll be lettin' you enjoy the rest of your evening." Mr. Doyle lifts his pint and moves back to his table.

Brian's wanderings bring him back to our table, "How was everything? Is there anything I can get you?"

Karen and I reply in unison, "No, we're full."

Karen elaborates, "It was all delicious. Thank you."

I raise my glass, "I think I could manage another Guinness. I'm at least a two-pint man."

"I'll let me wife know you enjoyed yourselves. I'd better get back behind the bar; patrons are getting nervous about not havin' a drink before the band begins. I'll signal when your Guinness is ready. Thanks again for coming in."

As the band begins playing, many of the patrons sing along, and during various songs people raise their glasses and yell in unison, "Aye." I'm not sure if they are classic Irish ballads, band songs known to the villagers, or a local bar activity, but it's all great fun to be part of.

Movement at the front door catches my eye and my focus. Karen turns her head over one shoulder, then the other, "What are you looking at so intensely?"

I lean into whisper, "Don't turn around. Fionnuala Lynch just walked in. Brian looks pissed. Diedre looks as if she could cry."

"What do you think it is? Could Fi be the 'one Brian is steppin' out with?'"

"I don't know. Brian just motioned Fi onto the back hallway. He grabbed her arm, but she pulled away. If my lip reading is correct, Brian is saying things like, 'you,' 'no,' 'bitch,' and the 'F' word. Now she's poking her finger into Brian's chest."

"Do they need someone to diffuse the situation?" Karen asks.

"No. Brian just grabbed Fi again and when she pulled away, she almost fell over. She's leaving now."

Fi storms past the bar. There's a break between songs from the band, and the entire room hears her say, "You ruin everything!"

I focus back on Karen, "That was intense. I'm glad nothing ever happens in the village except a drunken argument."

Karen lowers her shoulders, "You'll have to tell me everything when we get home."

The band begins its second set. The music continues on and off until the early part of the morning. Karen and I close down the bar. I ask Brian if there's anything I could help him with, but he declines. Deidre's shoulders slump and Brian looks as though he's chewing on something. They look relieved as we put our jackets on and step out into the cold, misty night, or should I say morning air.

Karen exclaims, "We closed down the pub!"

"Yeah, I can't remember the last time we did that."

"This is what we promised ourselves in retirement. We can stay out late, sleep in the next day. You don't have to worry about a call from the police department."

"I can drink beer!"

"Really? That's it? You can drink beer."

"I'm not drunk, but I have a good 'buzz' and the car is parked at home."

We're only a few feet from the Lamb and Ram when I hear a car door slam shut.

A yellow 2003 Citroen Saxo that was parked next to the pub starts up. I see the rear taillights illuminate and the car backs out the drive. It's dark so I can't see the driver. I know that no one else was in the pub when we left so it'd have to be Brian or Deidre. The car almost hits the end of a fence and heads out to the east. I'm curious where someone would be going at this time of the night. My first thought would be an emergency. I hope nothing is wrong. I make a note of the make and model and promise myself to clarify the owner of the vehicle the next time I'm in town. Professional curiosity never dies.

Chapter 6

"You've eaten through a whole chicken, two loaves of bread, and a pot of jam," Karen exclaims.

"Nobody says 'pot of jam'."

"They do in Ireland, I think." Karen smirks.

I laugh, "Yes. Yes. I have. And it feels good not to be eating on the run. Sandwich in one hand, semi-warm cup of coffee in the other, heading from call to call. How about a provisions trip?"

"Does it include some form of bakery as well as the grocery store? I'm craving a muffin or something sweet this morning."

Wiggling my eyebrows at Karen, "Something sweeter than me?"

Karen smiles and feigns shyness, "Nothing could ever be as sweet as you."

I pull Karen into a hug, "Yes, whatever you want."

"Dan, grab the laptop, please. I need to pay bills on-line and transfer some money. We can stop at the coffee shop and hook up to their signal."

"Oh good, coffee!"

Karen shakes her head and laughs, "Okay. Soon all you'll have is a two-word vocabulary: *beer* and *coffee*." The walk into town is damp and slightly windy, our shoes squeak on the slate walk, and our coat edges snap in the wind. The sky looks foreboding.

As we pass Fi's office, she comes out of her office, "I have the particulars about the party next Saturday!" Her emerald green blouse flutters in the breeze, but the skirt, which could be painted on, refuses to be disturbed by the wind. It's only when she walks, that it sways and bunches around her hips. It seems too sexy an outfit for the office. The beads hanging from her ears are shiny in the daylight and the necklace across the blouse, moves with the rise and fall of her breasts. Nothing cheap about her jewelry. She hands me a beautifully hand-written invitation that reads:

The Laird Arthur O'Connor
requests the honor of your presences at the Autumn Festival,
the 14th day of September this year of our Lord
at 7 p.m. at Baile Manor.
R.S.V.P. regrets only.

The weight and texture of the invitation are impressive. The ink looks painted on, it's so black. I look at Fi and reply, "Please inform the Laird that Karen and I have every intention of attending."

"I'm sure the Laird will be pleased to hear that. Personally, I'm happy you're coming," Fi says, holding my gaze.

"Is there anything that Karen and I can bring?" I say to break the moment.

"No. Laird O'Connor has the party catered."

"Is there any particular beverage that the Laird enjoys?" I continue.

"I know that each night before turning out the lights at bed time, Laird O'Connor enjoys a small glass of Jamison whiskey."

My curiosity is piqued about how Fi would be privy to that information. Fi blushes as if she realizes that she let a little-known secret slip. Then she tosses her hair and the earrings dangle in the movement. I let it go without asking further details. Karen and I thank Fi for the invitation and assure her we'll see her at the party. As Fi walks back to her office, I wonder if she's involved with Brian and Laird O'Connor, possibly simultaneously, or maybe alternatively. Is Fi the village flirt, or the village opportunist?

I notice Karen smiling at me, "What?"

"Really? You didn't notice her flirting with you?"

I pull my shoulder back and grin, "I've still got it."

"Oh, yeah. *I* like what I see." Karen replies, "That outfit she's wearing looks tailored to her. That's not some cheap, off-the-rack item. I saw it in the window at Le Meilleure."

"I noticed it fit her perfectly."

"I'm sure you did." Karen snickers, "I wonder if she's a regular customer of Claire's. So where does her income come from?"

"I don't know. Maybe it isn't *her* income she's spending. Her jewelry isn't cheap either. Curiouser and curiousier."

Karen and I finish our grocery shopping quickly and head over to the coffee shop.

The Second Byte Café is two doors down from the Lamb and Ram pub. I open the door to the warmth and aroma of freshly brewed coffee and the lingering scent of Brut cologne. Maybe John Shea gets his coffee here. The room has an eight-foot bakery display case filled with a variety of scones, rolls, and other desserts. Two large menu boards hang on the wall behind the case which lists coffees, mochas, cappuccinos, teas. There are several people: three teenagers giggle and point to a computer screen, then look around them and smother their comments with their hands. A woman in a shabby coat fiddles with her coffee cup and frowns at the screen on the computer in front of her. On the stool behind the counter is a thin man, bent forward to read his own computer, wispy brown hair with some scalp showing, horn-rimmed glasses, and a goatee. His clothes hang on him and bunch with his slump. My first thought says 'beatnik,' for lack of a better word, but again then I could be showing my age. The lines on his face give a "mid-fifties" age estimate. He looks up as we enter and says, without the slightest Irish accent, "Hello, can I get you anything?"

I look at Karen, whose intent study of the menu board and the case results in, "I'll have a medium caramel mocha and a cranberry scone, please."

I add, "And I'll have a large double Americano and a blueberry walnut muffin."

The man looks directly at us, holding out a handshake, "Welcome, fellow Americans. I'm Ralph Santini, originally from Chicago, Illinois."

I extend my hand, "I'm Dan Novice and this is my wife, Karen."

Karen looks at Ralph, "Nice to meet you. Dan, I'm going to find a table and start." I learned early in my marriage to avoid getting in the way of my wife's bill paying process. We understand that we rarely approach a problem in the same manner or with the same tactics, so it is best have "one crew chief and one line worker" for each task. Crew chief is in charge and line worker assists as crew chief needs. For paying bills and handling the current, short term financial needs, Karen is crew chief. For long term investments I'm crew chief. That idea has saved us from a number of angry incidents.

Ralph brings our beverages and pastries to the table, "May I join you?"

I motion to a chair, "Please." Karen focuses on the screen.

"I heard you're here for three months."

"Yes. We want to have time in a village and not just a tourist town. How'd you come to Ballyram, may I ask?"

"I was working for the City of Chicago when I hurt my back. I took my pension and early retirement about three years ago. I wasn't sure what I'd do next, but then an uncle on my mother's side called to see if I was interested in buying the coffee shop so he could retire. I'd been to Ballyram several times with my mother, visiting her family so I was aware of the village and the shop. I was divorced, no children, so I decided to sell everything and move here."

Karen tilts her head, "Are you happy here?"

"Most of the time. I taught myself to bake, expanded the menu, and haven't looked back. When the store next door became available I bought it too. I've always been interested in health food, so I thought I'd join the two ideas together. I sell vitamins, supplements, and organic foods, such as wheat germ and flax seed. Feel free to walk around next door."

I look at Ralph, "Your name sounds familiar, but I can't place how or why I should know it."

Ralph laughs, "I get that a lot. You must be a reader. I was named after the author Rafael Sabatini. He wrote the *Black Swan, The Sea Hawk* and *Captain Blood* in the early 1900s."

"That's it. I loved pirate stories when I was younger. I've read all of them."

"Yeah, he was my father's favorite author."

Karen finishes and closes the laptop. Ralph stands up. Shaking our hands, he smiles, "It was nice meeting our newest villagers and I hope to see you again."

As he walks away, Karen says, "That was nice." We continue eating in silence. The muffin I had was perfect. It has a sugar coated top and a moist body. I ask Karen about her scone. Karen rolls her eyes, happily squirms in her chair, and utters, "Um. Awesome! Maybe the best I've ever had. It has sweet dough but not too sweet. It was crisp, but not dried out and I can taste the cranberries, yum!!!"

I laugh, "Glad you like it. I think I may get another Americano." I signal to Ralph and explain what I need. He nods, gets to work, and then he looks up and out the window.

I turn and see Tim Clark, owner of the bakery, walking by. The overcast skies can create distorted shadows, but the look Tim casts as he peers in the window is pure anger. It's clear a storm is eminent. Ralph averts his eyes and tries to look like he is concentrating on making my coffee. No break in step, no gesture, and no words exchanged, but Tim's eyes focus on the window as he walks by.

When Karen and I are outside, I explain the situation I witnessed.

"Do you think there is some animosity between Ralph and Tim because they both sell bakery?"

"Maybe. I'd love to know the story behind it.

"So, would I," Karen whispers.

Later that evening a knock at the door brings me out of my occupation with my book. John Shea is at the door. He wears a deep purple shirt, open three buttons down, gold chains hanging around his neck, and the heavy scent of Brut.

"I'm sorry to be disturbin' you without calling first. I hoped

I'd find you at home and not out playing with the fairies." He winks and grins at me.

I have no verbal comeback. I just step aside as he wipes his feet and steps into the cottage. "Karen, John Shea is here." I call out.

Coming out of the kitchen, Karen stops in her tracks with her mouth open when she sees John.

Offering Karen, a potted plant, he says, "Hello, I'm John. I wanted an opportunity to stop by and welcome you meself. Is the cottage to your likin'?"

Karen shakes his hand and squeaks out, "It's beautiful . . . ummm, thank you."

I grin to myself. I should've met Karen in the kitchen and prepared her for this, but it was fun to see her face.

Her years of being a gracious host appear, "Please sit down. How very nice of you to think about us. Can I get you something to drink?"

John waves off Karen's invitation, "I don't mean to be imposin' on ya. Just wanted to be sure you'd settled in and were satisfied with the cottage."

"It's what I'd hoped for in an Irish cottage with all the modern amenities."

"Brilliant. Again, my apologies for not callin' first. I was just driven' by and took the chance you'd be home. Just a word of caution bein' out at night as the roads are dark and narrow. Not a lot of room for cars and people to navigate together.

"I've noticed that," I reply.

"If you have any problems in the future, please call. Have a good evening." John makes his way to the door.

After he leaves, I close the door and lean against it. Karen smiles, "Now I know what you mean about the 'Elvis thing' and the amount of cologne he wears. He seems like a nice man and it was good of him to check on us, but his look caught me off guard."

"I know, I saw your face," I say grinning. "It was perfect."

Karen's lip twitch with a smile, "You're naughty. Next time a little heads up, please. The begonia plant is nice, I guess."

Knitting my eyebrows together, "Is everything alright? Is there something wrong with the plant?"

"No. I'm sure it's nothing. Just being silly."

"About what?"

"Nothing. Forget I said anything. Let's enjoy our evening."

We settle onto the couch and just as I turn the T.V. on, there's another knock at the door. I knit my brows together, "Maybe John forgot something." I open the door to Quinn, "Hello."

Quinn shakes my hand, "Sorry to bother you, but I was in the area and thought I'd stop by to ask about when would be a good time to go over cases with you."

"Sure, come on in." Karen waves from the couch.

"Was that John Shea leaving?" Quinn asks.

"Yes, he stopped by to check if we're happy with the cottage," Karen replies.

"Well, just a friendly word of caution with him. Rumor has it that he was accused of managing a home improvement business, ended up doing some kind of dodgy deals in Dublin, so he had to move here and start over."

My curiosity piqued, "Was he indicted?"

Quinn shakes his negative, "No, the business said it didn't want any bad publicity, so they settled with him. What I heard is that Shea was fronting for the Irish mob and some rivals of the mob went missing. It's rumored the rivals are hidden in some of the 'projects' done by the business. The business didn't want that information getting out. That's when he quietly moved here."

Raising my eyebrows, "That's an interesting twist. Any trouble since he's been here?"

"Not a one. I'd like to get a look at his books. He and Fi both seem flush with cash. I've a good idea of how much they each make, but both have the best clothes and jewelry. I can't explain how." Quinn shakes his head, "I don't mean to disturb you. I thought if you could give me some days and times, then I'd pick out some cases to discuss with you."

Karen breaks in, "We're invited to Laird O'Connor's party. Could it wait until after that?"

"Sure. I know the party is tomorrow night. I'm off next Tuesday, if that'd work for you."

"Absolutely, Tuesday night you and I can go over a case or two. I look forward to it," I reply shaking Quinn's hand.

"Thank you so much. Until Tuesday night then. Enjoy yourselves and stay out of trouble," Quinn says with a laugh.

After closing the door, I turn to Karen, "That's interesting about John."

Karen snorts, "Yeah. Maybe then I'm not being silly about John's choice in plants."

"Huh?"

"Well, begonias can represent 'a fanciful mind' and he does like Elvis. But they can also mean 'be cautious.'"

"*That is* interesting," I muse.

We finish watching T.V and head off to bed.

Chapter 7

I'm dressed in my best attire and ready to attend Laird O'Connor's party. Karen is wearing the black crepe dress and jacket she purchased at Le'Meillure. We slip into our heavier, full-length raincoats and step into the cool evening air. The skies are cloudy, but as of yet no rain.

Irish road, no street lights, and moist dirt under our shoes. Karen and I walk to the Manor without difficulty. Despite the dampness, we slow our pace as we make our way up the curved, crushed gravel drive, pausing for a few minutes in front of the building to look at it. The Manor itself is an 18th century, Anglo-Irish type home, or should I say, *castle*. Stunning. The stone portico to the left of the Manor, is the first thing I notice. It adds a Gothicized quality to the Manor as I imagine carriages with the country's finest pulling in and being protected from the elements. Karen and I make our way under the portico to the massive, beautifully carved wooden door that stands eight feet high. A green shield with a crowned, gold lion standing on its rear legs is emblazed on the brass door knocker.

I turn to Karen, pointing to the door knocker, "Family crest?"

Karen shrugs her shoulders as a tuxedoed, elderly man answers the door. He escorts us into an impressive entry with a white marble floor and walls with twenty-foot high fluted marble columns that define three amazing arches. He takes our coats and informs us, "Everyone is in the Great Room, sir." Our shoes click on the inlaid marble motifs, we skirt some rugs, and I walk carefully around the waist high vase.

"That's a ginger jar," Karen whispers. "People used it to give the house entry a nice smell."

There are age-flecked mirrors with wide borders of gold. And then we come to the open double doorway of the Great Room.

It's entirely possible that the entire cottage we rented, including the garden, would fit in their Great Room. The room is 30 feet wide by 45 feet long. The ceiling is at least 20 feet high, and coffered. It's breathtaking. The walls are lined with a rich dark wood paneling. Three enormous chandeliers made of metal swords hang from the ceiling. Their hilts form the inner circle and their blades jut out to grand splendor. Lights between are simulated flame bulbs. If an armored clad knight burst into the room and shouted, "My Lord, we must be off to slay a dragon," I'd believe it. Ten or twelve wait staff in black suits and white shirts balance trays: some are filled with stem glasses, some with pilsners, their tops foamy. Other staff move through the room with trays of dirty glasses: a jumble of leftover food fragments and tiny plates. People laugh among the clatter of plate and glass, and an occasional bellow at a joke can be heard. Near the entrance I notice Fi. She's wearing a black dress with long sleeves and a neckline that shows a fair amount of cleavage, looking barer in contrast to her covered arms. Her hair is pulled up and held in place with silvery barrettes. Black pearl studs in her ears and a matching necklace rise over her breasts. Black beads, pink skin: Fi knows what will get a man's attention. She seems to be basking in the attention from a grey-haired man at her side, the man I suspect is Laird O'Connor. He may not be looking at cleavage, but a lot of other men are glancing her way.

Fi pats him on the arm and hurries over to us, “I’m so glad you both were able to make it. Please, let me introduce Laird O’Connor.” She turns, expecting we will follow her. Laird O’Connor is man of approximately 67 years old, 5’10”, 190 lbs, soft blue eyes and white hair that has thinned on top. He stops speaking to Harvey and Claire Clarke as we approach. “Laird O’Connor, may I introduce Daniel and Karen Novice.”

His Lairdship extends his hand to me, “Good of you to come. I’ve been anxious to meet my new tenants. The cottage is suitable, I hope.” He has few wrinkles, a low and even voice, a genuine smile.

“Yes,” I say.

“Brilliant. I hope Ireland is turning out to be the vacation you hoped for: sights, people, weather, not that there’s much I could do about the weather,” he says with a hearty laugh.

“Yes, we have enjoyed ourselves immensely.”

“What can I get you both to drink?” Laird O’Connor signals to a waiter.

“A pint of Guinness for me and a diet cola for my wife. Thank you for your generous invitation. Your home is magnificent.”

“Baile Manor has been in my family since the 1400s. The actual word Baile is Irish for ‘home.’”

“I’d be interested in hearing about its history.”

My family has had to defend it from various invading forces. I don’t know how much you know of Irish history or if you’re interested much. Our west wall did need repair after the British invasion of 1583, when the castle fell, and my family fled for a more temporary rural setting. The family did return several years later and has been in residence ever since. If you look closely, you'll still be able to see where the wall was repaired as the stone does not match, and there are divots on the remaining exterior walls from damage of gunfire." Laird O'Connor waves his hand toward the wall.

I'm in awe. "It's truly impressive."

"Thank you. Beware: there are ghosts here as is true of much of Ireland. The hundreds of years that my family has lived here, died here, given birth here—both with triumph and tragedy—have led to a number of family members and friends deciding to stay on. I and some of my guests have had encounters with the resident ghosts."

"Really? Who?"

"The most infamous ghost is a distant relative. The legend goes that about four hundred years ago one of my predecessors was a rogue, Sir Fergus O'Connor. He was said to have ruled the village with fear and intimidation for nearly a decade. He was a heavy drinker and had the nasty habit of taking young girls from the village back to the castle for his pleasure, without benefit of marriage. Although the villagers were often angered by Sir Fergus's actions, they felt powerless to stop him. The story goes that Fergus went hunting in the woods alone one morning and was found late that afternoon with an arrow through his back. He lingered in a delirious state for days. His attacker was never found. The local priest refused to allow Fergus to be buried on consecrated ground. The family feared Fergus's remains would be desecrated and had him buried in an unmarked grave somewhere on the property. It has been said that his spirit roams the halls looking for his murderer, especially during violent storms."

Laird O'Connor turns to a gentleman to his right and says, "Isn't that right, Father Kennedy, that Fergus was not welcome in the church cemetery?"

Father Emmet Kennedy is a small man, no more than 5'7 and 150 lbs., approximately 70 some years old with red rimmed, brown eyes and brown hair that forms a natural tonsure around the pale pink dome of his head. He is dressed in standard priest fare, collar and all.

Fr. Kennedy emits a nervous laugh, "I'm known to be old, but was not present during the time that Fergus was with us." The Laird bends with laughter. Harvey chuckles. Claire titters. Fr. Kennedy continues, "I understand that the local priest at the time deemed Fergus 'a social and moral wretch.' Being accused of crimes against God and humanity would've prevented Fergus from being buried on sacred ground."

Hoping to break the tension, I ask, "Is Fergus the only restless soul in the Hall?"

Laird O'Connor's eyes return to our small group, "When I was a boy, my great aunt spoke of a story from her youth. In 1915 she was eleven years old. She was sitting along the river that runs through the estate; she looked up to see her eldest brother, who was eighteen years old. She believed he had returned home from the battlefront of World War I. He was still in full uniform including his helmet and gun. My great aunt remembers crying with joy, kissing her brother's face, and happily talking to him of the plans she had for the two of them now that he was home. Her brother would only say, 'Take care my little one and always be happy. I can't stay. I'm needed elsewhere.' My great aunt thought it meant he needed to return to the war. Later that day the family received notice that their eldest son was killed two days earlier. My great aunt often remarked about feeling her brother's presence here, as he was to become the laird of the manor had it not been for his tragic death. My grandfather became laird of the manor as he was next in line." He stops abruptly and wipes a hand across his forehead, "I'm sorry to go on and on with my family's boring history."

I don't find it boring at all. I'm fascinated by the idea of living in a haunted castle.

"The Laird and Baile Manor are what hold the village together," Fi interjects. "You're part of history."

Laird O'Conner blinks and returns to the present. "I'm sorry for going on this way. Be sure to help yourselves to a plate of something from the buffet."

The selection and layout dazzle my eyes. There are three full-size banquet tables covered with beautiful lace-trimmed cream tablecloths that must be Irish linen.

Karen pauses, "This is amazing."

Nodding agreement, "I don't know where to start."

Karen turns to me and whispers, "The food looks so good I may need two or three plates. Is there a way to do that without looking like a pig?"

Karen winces when a slice of filet squashes the design on a pastry.

Finding a table, we're ready to lift the food to our mouths when two people approach and introduce themselves as Sean and Mary O'Neil. Sean is a stout man at 5'8 and well over 200 lbs. His hair and he have departed company, except for a few hardy strands that appear randomly on his head. Mary is a head shorter and considerably rounder. They ask to join our table. Harvey Clarke also pulls up a chair.

Fi stops by the table. Smiling, she leans into me, "Is everything to your liking?" Curious. It's like she's playing lady of the manor.

Karen breaks in, "Everything is amazing. The beef is delicious."

Fi's eyes sparkle, "You should taste one of Mary's recipes; she likes to use 'secret ingredients' in her creations. Only some of us have been let into those secrets." The smile that lifts Fi's face has an edge to it. So, does her voice. My coppy sense questions the meaning of Fi's statement and leaves me feeling wary of Fi's barb.

Karen states, "I'm not sure what you mean?"

Fi laughs, "Sean's a lucky man that Mary loves him as much as she does and it shows." As both O'Neils have quite round bodies, I'm wondering if Fi means they have close association with food.

Sean has his camera and says, "Can I get a group picture. I can give ya a small memento of your time in the village." He takes a picture of everyone at the table.

Suddenly it seems as if Fi snarls as she looks across the room. Her upper lip lifts and her eye narrow, making her usually wide-open eyes into slits. I look up as a stunningly beautiful, classic Irish beauty enters the room. She is striking at approximately 45-46 years old, at least 5'8 no more that 145-150 pounds with vivid red hair (natural?) and sky blue eyes. She is impeccably dressed in a black pantsuit, white blouse, and large emerald earrings.

Karen leans into me and says, "I suddenly feel underdressed."

It's meant to be an entrance, and the newcomer has succeeded in grabbing everyone's attention. Laird O'Connor's face lights up at her appearance. She makes her way to the Laird and all eyes are on her. I turned to ask Fi who this is, when a sudden brilliant strike of lighting is seen through the massive gothic windows, followed by a tremendous downpour of rain.

A high-pitched, short-lived sound can be heard. The lights in the Great Room flicker and then resume their former luster.

"Was that a tornado siren?" I question

Behind us I hear Sean's voice, high pitched and wavering, "The wail of the Banshee is never welcome."

"The wail of the Banshee?" I ask, "That's just an old Irish legend, but the particulars escape me. What exactly is the Banshee?"

Sean shakes his head, "The Banshee is a female spirit heard on the night when someone is about to die. She is an omen of death, a messenger from the Otherworld, as it were."

I can't stop myself, "Does she resemble the Grim Reaper?"

"No! Banshees are dressed in white with flowing hair. They can resemble a hag, but not always. Their wail is terrifying. If a Banshee is seen combing her hair with a silver comb, beware. Legend has it that no one should ever pick up a silver comb as it's a lure by the Banshee to call people to their death." Sean emphasizes.

"So, it's just a legend with no more power over life and death than any other ghost story," I say hesitantly.

His eyes flash with anger, "Don't be so quick to judge, boyo. When I was just a boy, I heard the Banshee wail outside my house, and the next day my dear mother died without warning."

"That has to be a coincidence. It can't be true, can it?"

Sean's voice lowers, almost to a growl, "There is much between heaven and earth we have yet to understand. Myths have been known to have their beginnings in truth."

I have a flashback to a college lit class, where an instructor reminded us that Shakespeare made the same comment.

Laird O'Connor raises his voice to carry across the ballroom, interrupting the murmurs of conversations, "Please let us get back to the party. I've asked the string quartet to play, but before that happens I have announcement to make. Many of you know that I lost my beloved wife to a desperate battle with cancer more than five years ago. I thought I'd never recover, that is until I met this amazing woman, Colleen Moore. I'd like to ask Colleen to please come up here. She has brought a light into my heart and soul, so I'm pleased to announce that Colleen has accepted my proposal of marriage."

There is a loud and harsh gasp behind me that cuts across the murmurs. Everyone turns toward our table, and I realize that it came from Fi. She's holding a wine glass with the stem snapped off. I witness something in Fi's eyes: anger, sadness, or jealousy. I think, maybe a little of all three. Mary twitters with laughter. I wonder if her reaction is happiness for Lord O'Connor or a response to Fi.

Karen leans into me and whispers, "I get the feeling there's a lot more to this story."

Fr. Kennedy stands next to Lord O'Connor. His voice sounds as though he's giving benediction, "Let me be the first to congratulate you and Colleen on this momentous occasion. Please everyone, raise a glass as we say 'Best Wishes' to the happy couple.

Glasses and voices are raised in a toast. I glance across the room to see if Fi has raised her broken glass in a parody of a toast, but I can't see her. I wonder if she's left the party. The quartet begins to play and people resume their conversations, glasses clink, and visitors browse the buffet. Slowly, the rain begins to lessen and finally stops.

Three hours later I smother a yawn: the quartet's final set has ended, and guests are moving reluctantly toward the door. The gold and bronze clock in the main hall chimes midnight. Laird O'Connor and Colleen are at the door thanking people for coming. Karen and I take this opportunity to introduce ourselves to Colleen and to wish her and Laird O'Connor all the best. He stops me and says, "I know you're a retired police detective from the United States. I was wondering if I might speak to you sometime soon regarding a recent concern I have."

"Certainly, what can I help you with?"

"Not now. The hour is late and I'll need some time to give you the details. I'll call on you in the next day or two."

"Is this something you should take to the local Garda?"

Laird O'Connor looks down, "This needs more advice than straightforward law enforcement action. Please don't trouble yourself now. I'll call you to set up a more appropriate time and place."

"I look forward to your call. Thank you again for the invitation. Good night."

"It has been my pleasure," he says, shaking my hand as Karen and I leave.

Once outside the gates of the manor, Karen asks, "What was that all about?"

"I don't know but I get the feeling Laird O'Connor is afraid of something or someone. I guess time will tell. I'll just have to wait for his call."

The night air feels very cold after the warmth of the castle. The road is muddy, and our feet slide slightly in ruts that formed as cars churned through the mud in the rainstorm's aftermath. There are no streetlights on this country road; it's so dark that I'm not able to see my hand in front of their eyes.

Karen is holding onto my belt and says, "Good thing you're in front to me, because if there's a crazed driver coming down the road, you would be able to sacrifice yourself to save me."

"Yeah, I'm always there for you, babe."

"Well, I'm sure you'd want to throw yourself in front of whatever danger there is. Even lions, or tigers, or bears?"

"Oh my!"

Karen giggles, "You do know where we're going, don't you?"

"Yes, dear, in the military I passed orienteering."

"Could you slow down, my feet are killing me."

"What were you thinking wearing high heels tonight?"

"My feet may hurt, but they look good with my new dress. Just remember that it doesn't matter what you do as long as you look good doing it!"

"But you don't wear high heels when walking on country roads."

Drily Karen replies, "Fine! Whatever!"

The journey home is slow and chilly, but the warmth of the cottage is a welcome respite. This cottage does feel like home as we both get ready for bed and crawl in, exhausted but content. The food and the conversation of the evening were tremendously satisfying. Tomorrow will bring a whole new day, I tell myself. Help the local Laird and maybe get a tour of the rest of the castle.

Chapter 8

Early the next morning, Karen and I decide to walk away from town and into the countryside. A second wave of rain swept through in the early hours of the morning. The air is cool with the smell of burning wood. Everything is damp. The shrubs leak water and the trees seem covered in wetness. Even the sky is the color of damp, grey wool. I feel damp and stale, the result of too late a night and too many goodies, leaving both of us restless today. But it was all worth it. We walk on the gravel shoulder to avoid the puddles and the muddy ruts. Karen is verbally revisiting the fun she had at the party last night. However, I continue to wonder what Laird O'Connor needs to speak to me about. I have a nagging feeling it's something serious. I try to dismiss the thoughts with 'Time will tell,' and then I see small white lights flickering along the tree line at ground level.

"What do think those lights are?" I ask.

"I'd say they're Will-o-wisps," Karen replies.

I'm completely mesmerized by the fast-moving flashes. I start to follow them down a narrow side road, but Karen grabs my arm, "Dan, don't follow them. If memory serves me right, they can be dangerous or lead a person to danger. Something like that." Suddenly they disappear into the trees. My thought is broken by Karen, "Did someone hit an animal?"

I notice something at the end of the road of one of the side roads. It could be the dark fur of an animal, or even a bundle that fell off a truck.

"Maybe someone hit a deer. Are there deer in Ireland?" Karen asks.

A few steps closer and no, I've seen this before: it's a body. "Freeze!" I say louder than I had intended.

Karen jumps back, "What?"

"I doubt Irish animals wear tweed. It's a person."

"Who is it? Are they okay?"

Holding up my hands, "I can't tell who it is from this distance, but they're lying in the middle of the road. I doubt they're okay."

I glance at Karen and see her shoulders are rigid. I hear stress in her voice when she says, "NOT funny. What do you need me to do?"

"Stay where you are while I investigate closer. And please call for help." I hand Karen the phone.

"How do I call for help? 9-1-1 won't work here, will it?" Karen asks skeptically.

"I read in one of the guidebooks to dial 9-9-9 for the police or emergency medical help." I reply calmly.

"Seriously? Thank goodness you read stuff like that in a guidebook before we need it."

"Please just call," I insist.

There's a spattering of silver metal pieces, a broken headlight, and one bent length of yellow colored metal on the ground near the body. I step carefully around the metal pieces and bend down to feel for a pulse. People don't always look like themselves once they are dead, but I've met this person recently. It's Laird O'Connor. His arm is stretched out from his body, as though he had tried to wave after someone, or to signal for help. It appears he's the victim of a hit and run. On the other hand, there's a set of muddy tire tracks running from the side of the body, along the road. This happened after the storm then. Karen and I had told the Laird and Colleen goodnight shortly after midnight.

"Hello? Police, Garda?" Karen's voice on her cell phone sounds high and tense. She is trying to explain where we are and what's happened. I wait next to the body. I have done this way too many times in what I thought was a completed career. Laird O'Connor is lying face up, his eyes are open, and there's blood around his mouth and on the right side of his head. The smell of blood enters my nose. That dull bitter iron taste catches in the back of my throat and hangs there far too long. The tire tracks near his body are the width of a compact vehicle. The road is unpaved dirt about one and a half cars wide. No curbs. The tire marks indicate that the car hit the victim, made no attempt to veer prior to impact, but what's most alarming is that the tracks stop and reverse to back up over the victim. A set of tire marks goes squarely across the body. Bones broken, clothing torn, the arm and hand that remained next to the body flattened. I think one of the hardest things to view at an accident scene is how fingers are turned into broken bits. What used to use utensils, make music, write a name, is now blood and pieces of bone. A few hours ago, Laird O'Connor was wearing hand-tailored clothing and brown shoes with thick soles. Now one of his feet has a shoe and the other is turned backwards, wearing only a torn sock. The shoe is ten feet away, on its side.

My eyes catalog this and my mind compares it to other accidents I have investigated. Fifteen minutes later the police arrive. Peter Quinn is the first on the scene. Pictures taken record evidence and the officers take notes. Measurements are written down and debris bagged and tagged.

Quinn closes the door on the police wagon as the body is removed for autopsy. He turns to us and shrugs, “What can you tell me?”

Karen and I are questioned regarding the scene, and a half an hour later we are free to go.

“I want to go home,” Karen says. “I don’t want to be a tourist today.”

“Is that home home, or back to the cottage home? Airfare is expensive.”

Karen smiles.

Hugging her, I say, “Listen, I’ll join you later at the cottage. You okay?”

I know she’s going to be okay: Karen’s tough and smart. Karen gives me a weak smile, “Can’t stay out of an investigation, huh?” She turns back toward the cottage while I turn to Quinn.

Quinn and I are reviewing the scene when Tim Clarke appears on the scene.

“Tim, what are you doing here?” Quinn questions.

Tim’s eyes are dark with anger, “I heard there was an accident here, and I came to see for meself who it was. Not who I thought it would be, but this one will do!”

I open my mouth to ask something, and then close it. This isn’t my investigation.

However, Quinn does ask, “What does that mean?”

“This ‘Grand man,’ who everyone in town talked about as the ‘benefactor of the village’ with all his generosity, never stops his evil ways. Well, someone stopped him. Of that I'm glad."

Quinn puts up his hands, "Tim, I don't understand what you're sayin.' What are you talkin' about?"

"He raped me daughter," Tim spats out angrily.

My head snaps up. Quinn continues, "When, where?"

"This beast took me Moira. He took her sweetness, her trust, and then threw her away. He had no regard for the consequences of his actions on her. Now she's dead because of him. May he have suffered before his end!" Tim spits in the direction of the accident.

"Tim, I need to ask if you had anything to do with this accident?" Quinn asks quietly.

"You actually think this was an *accident*? You're stupider than that eejit Foley," Tim states and turns to leave.

"We're not done here," Quinn calls out.

A smirk crosses Tim's face, "I didn't have anything to do with this. But I'm not sad it happened. You want to talk to me more, then caution and charge me," he says as he walks slowly toward the village.

Quinn shakes his head in disbelief, "What was that? Well, I'll be talking to him more. Let's finish with the scene."

After an hour of more pictures and more measures, Quinn wraps up the scene.

"If you need help, I'd be willing to assist. I've reconstructed a fair number of crash scenes," I offer.

Quinn gives me a quick nod, "Thanks. I'll meet you back at your place later tonight."

It's another hour before I'm back at the cottage. Karen sits on the couch with a small blanket over her shoulders and ponders,

"We left at midnight and found him before 7 a.m. Who or what would entice him out? What was Lord O'Connor doing out early this morning after that late night at his home."

"I don't know, but it's suspicious, especially after his statements as we were leaving last night. I doubt it would have been a morning stroll. It was barely light out when we left the house, and he was cold when I felt for a pulse. Maybe tomorrow I'll stop in to see if Quinn's learned anything more."

Karen notes, "I feel we're part of this investigation, now." She snuggles up to me. I kiss her on the top of her head.

The rest of the day is spent at home, eating leftover stew with slices of brown bread, and watching old movies. The mood is solemn. It has gone from party to funeral in a matter of hours. My mind is racing with the scene from this morning.

Later that evening, Quinn stops by, "I'm sorry to be botherin' you. When I asked you about running scenarios, I had no idea something like this would happen."

I wave him in, "Please come in."

"I'm waiting for the post mortem report and I couldn't remove the evidence, but I was able to download pictures of the scene and all the measurements. Would you have some time to walk through what we have so far?" Quinn's eye search between my face and Karen's for signs of approval.

Karen laughs, "I'll make a pot of coffee. Quinn, have you eaten dinner?"

Quinn shakes his head negatively.

"I'll make you something while you and Dan go over the case." She says as she moves to the kitchen.

Quinn and I go through the pictures and make notes. Karen

brings a plate of scrambled eggs and toast. Quinn tucks into the food as if someone's trying to take the plate from him.

I look Quinn in the eyes, "I have to tell you that last night as Karen and I were leaving Laird O'Connor's party, he mentioned that he wanted to talk to me about a 'recent concern' he had."

"What was his concern?" Quinn asks.

"I don't know. I asked what I could help him with, but he downplayed it and said he'd call me in a day or two. I feel bad that I didn't press him for more details."

Quinn shakes his head, "You had no way of knownin' that this would happen. Thanks for the information."

"Also, Sean O'Neil talked about the fact that during the party, in the midst of the thunderstorm, he heard the wail of the Banshee. I don't believe in legends or such, but he sounded convinced, unless he was setting something up. I thought you should know."

"Sean does believe in the legends, myths, and ghosts. I'm more inclined to think that's what he thought he heard, but I'll follow up with him to see if he has an alibi. Thanks." He gives me a weak smile.

"Tim Clarke's statements also needs following up on. That was one angry man!" I say.

Quinn nods in agreement, "I knew Tim was sad, but I've never seen that level of anger before. What about his comment that 'This isn't the one I expected.' Who'd he think the victim would be?"

"I don't know. Does he think there'll be more victims? Was the wrong person killed? Do you have a list of suspects?" I ask. I tell Quinn about the conversation I overheard at Doyle's grocery store between two men and something going on in the village.

"You have no idea who was talking or what they were talkin' about?' Quinn inquires.

"I couldn't swear to whom the voices belong," I admit.

"Well, there seems to be more questions than answers at this point. I could use help on this, if you'd be willin.'"

Karen laughs, "Dan would love to help. He's very good."

I add, "Just a few days ago, Karen and I had a run in with the farmer at the end of the lane here. I'm sorry I don't know his name."

"If it's the one I'm thinkin' of, that'd be Charles O'Leary," Quinn says.

"Well, he made some angry remarks about 'the grand man getting his land' and having 'surveyor guys around.' I didn't know what it meant at the time, but given the fact that Laird O'Connor is dead, he may be another interview."

"Okay, I'll add O'Leary to the growing list."

"There seems to be a number of issues going on. It's like a Shakespearean play. There's anger, revenge, blame, and hurt."

We go about making a list of possible suspects and looking over the photos. The last thing we do is diagram the scene. Quinn reads each measurement to me and I plot every piece of debris collected from the road and the vicinity onto paper. We use a stone wall as a reference point. Deep tire tracks at the entrance to the lane indicate acceleration. I help Quinn with the equation that determines speed of the vehicle. Where Laird O'Connor's shoe landed versus the placement of the body calculates to a speed of 40-45 miles per hour. Laird O'Connor was thrown nearly 80 feet. Tire tracks across the back of the body lead me to believe that he realized what was happening and turned to try and escape. The ruts near the body reflects severe braking after hitting him, but the most disturbing point is that the car was backed up over the Laird as a second set of muddy tire tracks are visible on the body.

Quinn lets out a slow whistle, “Someone had every intention of killing Laird O’Connor. This was no accident.” I nod my head in agreement. Karen brings more coffee and cookies. We eat in silence as our eyes flick over the scene lain out in front of us.

Quinn stands, shakes my hand, “Thank you for your help. I didn’t realize crash scene investigation was this complex. And thank you for the hospitality. It means a lot to me. I was wondering if you’d be willin’ to help me with this investigation?”

“Are you sure? I’m a retired detective, but not a retired Garda detective.”

“It’s not official and would be unpaid.” Quinn eyes flick between mine and Karen’s faces before saying, “But this is a big case and me first. Sergeant Foley is retirin’ at the end of the month, so my superiors expect me to solve this.”

I look at Karen, who’s smiling and nodding.

“I’ll help any way I can, and I’m not worried about being paid. Why is Foley retiring? He doesn’t seem that old.”

“Brilliant. There are two rumors goin’ around. One is that Foley told administration exactly what he thinks of them and they suggested he should retire.” *Internal police politics are the same in any country, apparently.* “Two is that Foley messed up one too many investigations and bosses were tired of covering for him, so they suggested he retire.” Quinn shrugs.

“Which do you believe?” I ask.

“It’s not my place to judge,” Quinn states flatly.

I close the door behind Quinn and look at Karen.

"It's been a long day. I'm ready for bed. What about you?" She asks. I nod wearily.

Karen and I head off to bed. I find myself restless. It's hard to let go of my visions of the accident and what Lord O'Connor might have thought in his final moments. Who would have the level of anger it took to commit this crime? I vow to help Quinn find out.

Chapter 9

The sun is just coming up on a new day. I'm sitting in the living room when Karen comes out of the bedroom. Her hair is mostly held up with a barrette, she has no make-up, wears white athletic socks, faded black sweat pants with a hole in the knee and a fleece pullover. My face must have said it all because she looks at me and says, "What?"

"Do you feel okay?"

"No! I barely slept at all. I was up two or three times during the night; something about the scene yesterday was wrong, but I can't quite figure out what. Is it something I saw, I didn't see, or I heard? The scene kept racing through my mind and when it was about to come to me, the idea just slipped away. It's so frustrating. What I do know is that the Will-o-Wisps were true. They signaled danger."

I can feel my heartbeat picking up. Whatever Karen is searching to remember is going to be the key, I know it.

"I need caffeine. Did we remember to buy diet cola?" Karen asks.

"Oops. No. We didn't go into town yesterday after the scene in the morning."

"Okay, I think a walk to town is in order. I could go like this right now or I could go into the bathroom and attempt to look human."

"I'll wait for you."

Twenty minutes and my third cup of coffee later, Karen appears bathed, dressed, hair brushed, and make-up on. "I'm ready."

"You're beautiful. I'm sure there are many men who would want you!"

"Thank you."

The day is a bit overcast. As we walk I wonder how the Laird's death will affect the village? Just as we arrive in town, Sean O'Neil pops out of the restaurant, as if waiting for us to arrive and asks about the accident because we were there. His face is creased, and his shoulders are more bent than at the party last night. He has dark patches under his eyes, as though he wears a pale purple eyepatch. Nothing like a small village for everyone to hear or know or think they know everything in record time.

"I heard his Lairdship was hit by a passing car." He looks at me knowingly and says quietly, "The cry of the Banshee is never wrong. What can you tell me about the accident?"

Experience has taught me it's better to learn what others know before revealing what I know. I tend to be vague in my statements. I don my best blank expression and say, "I'm not sure what happened. The police are being very tight lipped about their investigation. What do you think?"

Sean shifts back and forth, and whispers, "Girl trouble. You see the Laird was bit of a rogue like his ancestor, Fergus. However, the Laird knew where his bread was buttered, as they say, but the rumor is his eyes, and other parts of him roamed even during his marriage. Since his wife died, he's been free to roam far and wide. I've heard that himself has been shagging women from here in the village all the way to Dublin. I'm guessing that a few women would've been offended to learn of his pending marriage. I heard the announcement was covered last week in the Dublin newspaper."

"What do you mean where his 'bread was buttered?'" I ask

His eyes widen and his hair floats around his head as he turns quickly, "That's right, ya wouldn't be knowin.' The Laird's first wife was the money in the relationship. However, her illness used up nearly everything they had. I've heard that the Laird is nearly broke and that's the reason for the marriage to the Moore woman. Laird O'Connor had the title and the respectability, but no money. She has plenty of money, enough to buy the title and the respectability. She could do worse than being Lady O'Connor. I'm sure the Moore woman knows she would never take the place of the first Lady O'Connor."

"I don't know what you mean?"

"The first Lady O'Connor was just that: all lady. A finer soul was never born. The Laird and Lady weren't without their troubles. It was terrible to see the Lady suffer the way she did."

"Oh, interesting. Well, it was nice to see you again. Please excuse us." Sean's face crinkles with disappointment at my lack of gossip. He shrugs one shoulder and excuses himself back to the restaurant.

"Karen, I'll just be a minute at the police station, if you're willing to get what we need at Doyle's."

Karen puts her hands on her hips, "You know it's going to be more than a few minutes but go."

My feet hurry as I approach the Garda station. It's slate grey stone block construction, two-story, Georgian architecture.

It's set back from the road with six parking spaces in front of the building. There are two squad cars parked. A classic black lamppost, with a Garda emblem outlined in white against its blue glass fixture, stands at the entrance.

When I enter the building, there is an imposing wooden counter, nearly four feet high. An officer sits behind the desk on a high wooden backed chair. I ask the officer if I could speak with Sergeant Quinn.

I ask, "How's it going?" when Quinn walks slowly out of one of the doors. His eyes are bloodshot and his tie is open and pushed to one side of his uniform shirt.

Quinn whispers, "I'm not sure. Laird O'Connor was much loved in this village and the higher ups are asking the same thing. I have the crime scene photos and all the evidence bags. The headlight that was found at the scene was analyzed, and it's from a 2003 Citroen Saxo with yellow paint on it. I know of one person in the village who drives that make and model. It's Brian Flynn, owner of the Lamb and Ram. Care to accompany me to see what he has to say?"

"Are you sure? I'm a civilian now."

"I'm sure. A second pair of eyes and ears can't hurt. Of course, if anything does go wrong I could just blame you." He grins, "Americans. Can't keep their eyes and ears to themselves, ya know."

"It's good to have a plan. Sure, I'd love to go with you. I walked into town with my wife. She's at the grocery store. Let me just tell her what's up. I'm sure she'll be fine with it . . . I hope!"

I run over to the store and find Karen with a basket of groceries and a carton of diet cola. I tentatively say, "Quinn asked me to join him while he speaks with a person of interest in the hit and run. Do you mind if I go? Will you be okay dragging all this stuff home?"

Karen sighs, "Of course, you're interested in this investigation." After a long pause while she looks into my face, a sly smile crosses her face, "Go, I'll be fine. I'll meet you at home, expecting an update."

Peter Quinn is in his cruiser and signals me to get in. We drive the short distance to Brian Flynn's home, which is above the Lamb and Ram. Quinn rings the doorbell and Deidre Flynn answers the door. "Good morning, Peter."

"Sorry, Dee, I'm here officially. Can we come in?" Deidre flattens herself against the door to allow Quinn and me into their tiny kitchen. It's spotlessly clean. Various types of countertops delineate work areas: Butcher block for meal assembly, a marble top area to roll out those delicious pie crusts, and stainless steel next to the stove to safely place hot pots and pans, all well-worn. The furniture is mismatched and worn out. Pots and pans appear to occupy every available space. The room smells of comfort food, rich gravy, and warm bread.

"Is Brian at home?"

"Yes, but not feeling well at the moment. Is there something I can do for you?"

Quinn slowly shakes his head from side to side, "No, I need to be speakin' with Brian. Is he hung over again? Go wake him up, please."

Deidre leaves and we can hear her. "No, I don't know what they want. Yes, you DO need to get up. Where's your trousers? How would I know."

Quinn looks at me and shrugs slightly. I give him that 'What are you going to do' look. A few minutes later, Brian appears in the doorway. He looks as if he's had a terrible night. He's pale with bloodshot eyes that stare at the floor but not at us. Then he shakes his head and blinks, focusing on Quinn. His clothes appear to be the ones he wore the day before, his hair is a tousled mess, and he smells a sour mixture of beer and body odor. When I was a new patrol officer, arresting my first drunk, my training officer said, "Once you smell a drunk, it's a smell you never forget." Irish drunks smell like drunks back home.

Quinn asks Brian," Where were you the night Lord O'Connor was killed?"

"Here. I'm always here. I own a business that keeps late hours. Me last three customers will tell you I was here until closing. Two a.m. Why?"

"Then you haven't heard. Laird O'Connor was struck and killed last night by a vehicle, much like the one you drive." Deidre opens her mouth as if to say something, and then quickly closes it.

Brian's eyes close and open slowly. He touches the counter behind him, "Well, I didn't do it. Why would I want to kill Laird O'Connor? I'd no argument with him."

"I don't think you meant to kill him. Brian, everyone in the village knows that when you get drunk, you drive fast and reckless. We need to see your car. Where is it?"

Brian angrily looks at me and without turning back to Quinn asks, "What's he doing here? He doesn't need to be knowin' this."

Blandly, Quinn replies, "He's keeping me company. Where's the car?"

Brian stumbles out the door and puts his hand against the faded siding to steady himself. Quinn and I follow to a gravel parking area on the side of the house. There backed into the parking spot is a 2003 yellow Citroen Saxo, with the right front headlight broken out and damage to the right fender. Quinn sighs. Brian turns to us with his eyes distended and his eyebrows climbing toward his hairline. “That wasn’t like that when I went to bed last night. I swear! You have to believe me. I didn’t go driving last night, I swear!”

“Do you remember going to bed last night or were you so drunk you blacked out?” Quinn inquires.

“I went straight to bed right after closing last night. Ask Dee.”

“Brian, we all know you’re your own best customer. This looks bad for you. I’m gonna need to take you in for further questioning.” Quinn provides Brian with his “rights” or “Caution” and places Brian in handcuffs into the back of the police cruiser. I take this opportunity to question Deidre, “Did Brian leave home at all last night?”

“No, I’m sure he didn’t.”

Deidre doesn’t make eye contact. Her voice is a whisper. I’ve the sense that she’s lying, but why? Is it to protect her husband, herself, or someone else entirely?

“Tell me, Deidre, was Brian here all night?”

“The truth is he passed out at approximately 2 a.m. I’ve learned that it’s best to leave him where he falls. Last night he fell in the kitchen of the pub. I just went to bed.”

“Is that it?”

“I felt him crawl in bed about 4 a.m., but where he was between 2 and 4, I can’t say for sure.”

I wander outside and meet up with Quinn. "Having the car towed back to the station?" Quinn nods affirmatively.

Some things don't change, no matter what the country. We stand silently, both looking at the car when something strikes me. The car is parked perfectly, wedged between the pub and a fence. There's approximately two to three feet clearance on each side, almost symmetrical. Quinn notices what I'm staring at and says, "Seems a little convenient doesn't it?"

I nod, "You mean that it's parked so well for someone so drunk that he can't remember running over someone. Not only that, he backs into a tight space with the damage to the car pointing toward the street for the whole village to see?"

"Yeah, something like that. It just doesn't look right, but for now I don't have another explanation. Let's get back to the station and question Brian further. At least this will give my supervisors something to talk over while we investigate."

Universal response, I think. The administration wants easy, quick answers. I second Quinn's feeling that it's just too easy.

Quinn and I drive back to the station silent. Brian continues to repeat that he's done nothing wrong. It seems we both believe in Brian's innocence, but how to prove it? It's Brian's vehicle with corresponding damage and he has no memory. When was the car taken? Why Brian's car? Was the car just convenient or meant to incriminate Brian? Who has a grudge against Laird O'Connor and/or Brian? Is this part of a larger plan? Should we be concerned that another situation is pending—another murder might be coming—or was this just an accident?

At the station, Brian is placed in an interrogation room. Quinn and I sit across the table. Quinn again cautions Brian, but he declines an attorney. I think the man is too hungover, too innocent, or too stupid. Take your pick.

Brian looks at Quinn and nods toward me, "Does he have to be here? He's not one of us."

"Humor me, Brian, and let him stay. I think he could be an asset as a trained investigator, and he can't do any more harm to the case against you."

Brian drops his head, "Why is this happening. I've never had a cross word with Laird O'Connor. It makes no sense." Quinn lowers his head to try and make eye contact, "There's a rumor that Laird O'Connor and Deidre had an affair, or at least that His Lairdship was interested in Deidre."

Brian's head heaves upward and his eyes snap with anger as he spits, "Who'd ya hear that from? I'm sure it was that cow, Maeve. It's a lie!! Deidre would never!!"

For several hours, we question Brian and finally Quinn terminates the interview because as Brian is unable to provide any new information. He's is moved to a cell for the night.

Quinn and I drive to the coroner's office where Quinn identifies me as his assistant, and we are ushered downstairs to the morgue; morgues all over the world must all be in the basement. We wait in a dimly lit hall painted a dirty powder blue and smelling of a combination antiseptic and old vomit. A door opens ahead of us and a woman of medium height, gowned and masked, tells us to come in, while pointing to baskets with booties and masks and telling us we must put those on. Trying to fit the snug stretchy slippers over my feet is a failure in proportion to my foot size. They rip but they're on. Good enough for government work. Once inside the autopsy room, Quinn introduces me to Coroner

Dr. Ian Smyth. He's a short, fat man with scraggly white hair sticking out from under an ill-fitting blue paper cap, and stains are scattered across his medical smock.

Laird O'Connor's body is laid out on the autopsy table of brushed stainless steel that could have been a sous chef's prep table except for the lip around its edge and the channels leading down to a drain at one end. Broad bruising across the chest, legs, and arms is evident. Bones protrude on his Lordship's right femur and clavicle. A tire wide depression is found horizontally the length of the back of the victim's skull. Dr. Smyth leans up against the wall, holding a roast beef sandwich in his left hand and says, "No doubt. Even without the tire tracks on his clothing. No doubt a'tall. Based on the extent of his injuries, it appears that Laird O'Connor was struck and indeed also run over. I can tell you that the first impact stunned him, breaking his rib cage and right leg, but the second impact delivered the fatal blow. Based on his blood alcohol content, he may not have been able to assess the extent of the situation or able to move too fast. Not drunk, but definitely impaired. The marks on his clothing do lend themselves to a scenario of someone hitting Laird O'Connor, stopping, and backing up over him."

I look at Quinn and say, "Someone wanted to be very sure Laird O'Connor was dead at the scene. Who'd be so angry or cold-blooded?"

This earns me a measured look from the coroner who excuses himself. Quinn nods at me.

This was very long day, I head home. As I walk through the door, I see Karen is starting to prep for dinner. "How was your day, Detective?"

"I'm not sure. There's something wrong. Something missing that shouldn't be missing. I know it's close at hand, but I can't seem to reach it. You've been home all day. I'm taking you out."

"We could try Foley's, the other pub in town." Karen brightens up.

I open the door to the pub. It's smaller than the Lamb and the Ram, smells different too, not bad, just a different whiff of ale and food combination. It's one large room that's wider than it is deep, with the bar at the back of the room. Several tables lie between the door and the bar. A number of different conversation fill the air, and two serving people shuffle and weave among the tables. Karen points to a couple of open seats at the bar. Making our way through the room I see several familiar faces. Karen smiles and waves at Maeve and Kathleen.

At the end of the bar is a wiry man wearing a green apron, one hand on the beer tap. He smiles and says, "What's it tonight?" I order a Guinness for myself and a diet cola for Karen. The bartender hands me two menus as he taps my Guinness. As the beer rests, he introduces himself.

Extending his hand, "I'm Michael and welcome to Foley's." He's about 35 years old, stands 5'8" or so with a great swath of dark hair swept from the left ear over the top of his head and intense brown eyes.

I return the introduction.

Michael asks, "And where ya be from and where ya stayin'."

I explain where we're staying. Michael snorts a laugh, "Have you had the pleasure of meetin' Brian Flynn of the Lamb and The Ram?"

I nod.

"Well, here at Foley's we have better beer, food, atmosphere, bartendin' and anything else that Brian Flynn may think of himself and his pub."

Trying to add some humor, I say, "I can see you and Brian aren't mates."

A smirk creeps across Michael's face and he crosses his arms over his chest, "Won't be long before you'll be knowin he's a lying and cheatin' drunk. Especially since he stole my girl, Fionnuala Lynch. I loved her deeply, but before I knew it she was ravin' about how wonderful Brian was and them bein' a couple. Her heart was broken when he suddenly tried to act all respectable and a family man. I'll be saying no more about that good-for nothin."

I set the menu back on the bar and ask, "Can we order?"

Michael drops his head and laughs, "Yes. Your lovely wife and you are guests at Foley. Not needin' hear my problems. What can I get you?"

Karen and I both order the Fish N' Chips.

Michael steps into the kitchen. "What do you think Michael was saying about Brian?" I ask. Karen shrugs her shoulders.

Several bites into our dinner, Karen leans into me and says, "I don't want to add insult to injury, but the food at the Lamb and Ram is better."

I nod in agreement. Karen and I finish and pay the bill.

Michael stops over, "Again my apologies and hope ya will return soon."

As we walk home, I roll my thoughts over and over in my head as well as the statements Michael Foley made.

I suddenly hear Karen say, "Hello."

"I'm sorry. Have you been talking to me and I wasn't listening?"

"YES! Do you think what Michael Foley said about Fi being his girl were true?"

"Well, he seems to think she was."

At home we watch television. At least Karen does. Karen announces she's ready for bed. I join her, but sleep is not easy.

Chapter 10

The next morning Karen tells me, "I had the weirdest dream. It's night. I'm walking down the road when I see Laird O'Connor waving to me on the side of the road and pointing to his right side, but as I get closer I see he's bleeding from his head. There's a figure dressed in black standing next to him and I fear it is the banshee. Laird O'Connor is still waving and smiling. The banshee is combing her hair and pushes him down. He reaches out for her, but she pushes him again and he stops moving. I start to run down the road toward him when Brian Flynn's car races past me and the banshee's comb flies out of the window. I stop running and stare at the comb, which transforms into . . . that's when I jumped awake. I've the feeling I should know what the comb means, but the answer eludes me."

"Party or no, I should have pressed Laird O'Connor to elaborate on what he was concerned about. If I'd been more insistent, then maybe this situation could have been avoided or at least I would have a better direction to this investigation. I just can't shake this feeling of regret," I say.

"I think you're second guessing yourself. I know you'll figure it out." Karen smiles, "If it makes you happy, we'll go into the village and you can speak with Quinn. I'll meet you at O'Neil's when you're done at the station."

Hugging her, I say, "You're the best. Have I ever told you

what a lucky man I am?"

Karen laughs and gives me the 'talk to the hand' sign.

Quinn is reviewing the bags of evidence. The blood on the bumper of Brian's car is a match to Lord O'Connor. The thing that doesn't make sense is a piece of metal. Quinn finds the bag and we both stare at it. "Is it a clip from the car?"

Quinn shakes his head. "I don't know where it would be from."

The clip, for a lack of a better term, is approximately three inches long, narrow, and fairly mangled. It used to be something else, but what?

I ask, "Can we take all the evidence to the car being held in the impound lot." Small shards of glass are missing from the headlight and all the metal fragments seem to have a place on the car, even though the pieces are bent. Enough pieces are available to make the headlight a match for the damage on the front end of Brian Flynn's car. The only problem is the clip. I look at Quinn, "Is the clip even from the accident or present prior to the situation?"

"I don't know. But there's no weather-wear, so my hunch would be that it's connected to this situation."

Rubbing my chin, "We need to know if Laird O'Connor's death is an accident or deliberate? Who? Why?"

"Brian Flynn is first on the list of suspects, since his car was the instrument used to kill Laird O'Connor, but Brian had no clear motive unless the rumor of Deidre's affair with Laird O'Connor is true," Quinn states.

Looking at Quinn, I reply, "Is this situation nothing more than a horrible accident? My gut is telling there's more to this situation."

"A second person would be Fionnuala Lynch since the Laird was her employer, and if there is a motive there, it could be jealousy. But if the Laird dies, so would Fi's job."

I ask, "Would Colleen Moore have a reason? The night of the party she and the Laird appeared happy. Why was Laird O'Connor out at that time of the night and on that road? Why wasn't he in bed with Colleen?"

We both shake our heads hoping an answer dislodges, but nothing.

I suddenly realize that two and a half hours have elapsed since I dropped Karen off in town.

"Quinn, I need to leave, or you WILL have a murder on your hands and I'll be the victim."

"I plan to release Brian Flynn for now. I've asked Fionnuala Lynch to come in to answer questions day after tomorrow. Would you be interested in being present?"

Would I? That's a story I'd like to know more about. "Yes, but I gotta go." I show up at the restaurant and apologize for my tardiness.

"I'm shocked, shocked I tell you, that while on a case you lost track of time."

At O'Neil's, Nora introduces herself as Mary O'Neil's daughter and greets us at the door. She's about 22 years old with soft brown shoulder length hair that just hangs about her head with little style or shape. She has deep brown eyes, wears a completely formless dress that appears far too old for her age, and has a heavy smell of lily of the valley. She looks like she took her mom's clothes out of the closet by mistake.

Nora asks, "Are ya' the two Americans staying in town?"

"Yes, we are. I'm Dan and this is my wife, Karen," I say as Nora gives a weak smile and shows us to a table for two near a window with the sun shining through.

"Me stepfather and me act as hostesses to the restaurant while me mother's in charge of the kitchen."

The restaurant is a square room at the front of the O'Neil home. Ten square tables with two chairs each that can be configured to host 4 or more patrons and 2 round tables that can accommodate 6 persons each. It seems a large restaurant for this small a town, but then again, the pubs were bustling.

While handing us the menus, Nora quietly utters, "It's a terrible shame about Laird O'Connor. God rest his soul."

Karen and I reply in unison, "Yes, it is."

"The New Testament says, 'Those who live only to satisfy their own sinful nature will harvest decay and death from that sinful nature.'" Nora mutters more into the air than us.

Karen has a bewildered look on her face. She opens her mouth as if to say something, but nothing comes out.

I recover from my initial shock, "I don't know what you mean by that."

Nora leans over the table and whispers, "I was friends with Moira Clarke. Never a kinder soul lived and beautiful she was. Laird O'Connor, with his wicked ways, seduced her and took her to his bed. Moira was in love with him. After a time he told her that she had been fun, but that it was over. Crushed her heart, he did."

"Oh, how sad. What did Moira do?" Karen replies.

"So ashamed was she that she moved to England, where she died in a car crash. All alone. No friends. No family. Moira's mother went to an early grave because of it."

Karen looks on the verge of tears, “I feel so bad for Tim Clarke. That’s too much sadness. I hope that Harvey and Claire have been a support for him through all of this.”

Nora nods, “I think they try, but I don’t think he ever recovered. He puts his heart and soul into the village bakery. Maeve does her best to cheer him up, but the pain is there. I’m sorry to be goin’ on. I’ll give ya a few minutes.”

Karen and I look over the menu. Karen looks up, “What a terrible story.”

“Yes, it is. I can’t imagine living through that.”

“I think I’ll have some comfort food. Are you hungry enough to help me finish everything?” Karen asks.

“I always have your back.” I wink, trying to add some levity to the situation.

We sit at the table and unroll our napkins to find small pieces of colored paper with printed messages. The messages are titled either “Food for Thought” or “Conversation Starter.” Karen’s says, “Marriages are not made in heaven. They come in a kit and you put them together.”

Mine says, “An idea can turn to dust or magic, depending on the talent that rubs against it.”

Sean comes over to our table, “If you need anything, ask.”

Karen replies, “Thank you for the offer. The messages rolled in the napkins are a great idea.”

He replies, “Brilliant. That’s me wife’s idea as she is the ‘brains of the operation. I bein’ the ‘hired help.’ He winks. Mary comes out of the kitchen. She acknowledges us with a nod, but doesn’t stop at our table, and shortly disappears back into the kitchen. Sean follows her, while Nora takes our order. Karen orders Guinness and beef pie. I order a cheese burger because I'm missing a bit of home. When lunch arrives, we tuck in. Sean stops at the table to ask if we need anything else.

I say, "Give my best to your wife. Everything was wonderful." I notice Charles O'Leary is passing by the window. When I look back to Sean, he's looking at the floor. O'Leary is making a face that reflects pure anger. "What was that about?" I ask with concern.

Sean shakes his head, "About ten years or so, Charles' older brother was killed in an auto accident. Sgt. Foley investigated and determined the cause was driver error. Charles was convinced that it was a mechanical problem and the car dealer had sold his brother a damaged car. He accused Foley of being lazy."

I knit my eyebrows together, "Okay, but what does that have to do with you?"

"A few weeks later, Charles drove his tractor over Sgt. Foley's Garda vehicle while Foley was in it. Foley barely made it out in time. I witnessed the whole thing. Charles didn't swerve or even try to miss the car. He saw Foley and drove straight at him. I testified against Charles. He's never forgiven me."

"You did the right thing. Why's he angry with you?" I ask.

"I've known Charles all my life. He demands complete loyalty from his friends, no matter what."

Karen scrunches up her face, "He expects you to lie for him when he's deliberately trying to hurt someone?"

"No, but *that's* Charles. He believes his opinion is right. Anyone disagreeing with him is subject to his anger, forever."

My cop curiosity appears, "Were changes pressed?"

"Oh, yes. He got three months in prison and some years of

probation. He was also required to see a therapist for his anger issues."

All I can think is that it doesn't seem to have helped.

Sean claps his hands together, "I'm sorry. You didn't come here to hear about village squabbles. Is there anything else I can get you?"

Karen smiles, "No, thank you. It was all great." On our way out, I see Quinn.

"Hey, I was hoping to run into you. I have Tim Clarke coming for an interview. You want to watch?" Quinn looks at Karen more than me.

"I want to look at some of the other stores and will meet you at the police station, okay?" She says looking at me.

I hug her and give her a kiss on top of her head. At the station, Tim is already in an interview room. I let myself into the observation room.

Quinn sits across from Tim, "At the crime scene you made some very serious accusations against Laird O'Connor. Care to tell me more?"

Tim's eyes flash with anger, "They're not accusations. They're the truth. He raped me daughter. Not against her will but forcing lies on her. She was powerless. He had his way with her, and when he was done, he just walked away, as if she didn't matter. Her shame drove her away from this village. She died alone in England. It killed me wife, too."

"What lies did he force on her?" Quinn questions.

"That she was important and the only thing that mattered to him. That she was the answer to his loneliness and that rubbish," Tim snaps.

Calmly, Quinn folds his hands on the table in front of him, "How far would you go to avenge her and for that matter, your son, Paddy too?"

Tim lowers his eyes, his bottom lip starts to tremble, and tears roll down his cheeks, "Not far enough. I'm a coward. I've had all these thoughts of what to do to Laird O'Connor and Brian but was never brave enough to follow through. I let me kids down. I didn't protect them when they were alive and didn't do nothin' after they was dead." Tim's body shutters as he cries, "I'm useless." Quinn slides a box of tissue toward Tim and leaves the room.

He joins me in the observation room, "What do you think?"

"I find it hard to believe someone cold-hearted enough to calmly take Brian's car, run down the victim, back over him, leave the scene, and calmly park the car back at Brian's, would fall apart this easily.

Quinn sighs, nodding affirmatively, "I'm releasing him for now. I doubt he's a flight risk. We'll need to continue to investigate. The problem is that we're not running out of suspects. I had hoped to have eliminated more names than we have."

Quinn returns to the interview room, informs Tim that he's free to go, but to remain available for questioning. Tim blows his nose and shuffles out the door.

Karen is waiting in the lobby of the station, "Hey, how about we pick up some Chinese for dinner tonight, so we don't have to cook, and we can eat whenever we feel like it."

I hug Karen, "Thank you for being you."

"Partners all the way," she replies.

Chinese in hand, our walk home is silent except for shoes scraping on dirt. My mind is racing with thoughts of the crime, when I'm suddenly aware Karen is talking to me or maybe just herself.

Karen sighs, "Fields, farms, manor houses, sheep, cattle and trees. And green. The suggestion that there might be rainbows or magic around the next turn. Those lines of plowing with the puffs of sheep on the hillsides. And then that wiggle of grey stone for the walls. We could be in a postcard of Ireland. It's as if we are on a movie set. I want to stop and touch everything to be sure it's real."

"Not sure the cattle or sheep, or for that matter their owners, want us stopping and touching," I say.

"True. That's interesting what Sean said about Charles O'Leary. I told Maeve about the incident we had with him when he accused us of surveying his land. Maeve said that his wife must be a saint for staying with that 'eejit.'"

The angry farmer pops into my mind. Is he connected to the Laird's death? I realize that this place has deep wounds under the surface of a picturesque Irish Village.

Chapter 11

Sitting at the kitchen table with Karen, my teeth may be working on the bacon but my mind is still grinding away on yesterday's evidence, "I'll talk to Quinn. Maybe he can locate Laird O'Connor's son Michael and determine if he played a part in his father's death. Also, I'm wondering if Quinn can learn who may benefit from the Laird's Will and if there is a motive."

"I'm glad to hear you're retired . . . Detective," Karen smirks.

"I know I'm retired and should step away from this case, but something's wrong here. I don't know what it is, but I can feel it. I think with a little more time, with the evidence, and further interviews with various people, that a true picture will emerge."

We're having our mid-morning coffee. Karen looks up over the morning paper and smiles brightly, "What this case needs is a party!"

I stare blankly. Karen continues, "Eric, Megan, and Hannah will be arriving next week. We could have an Open House party on Friday night after they arrive, and it would give us an opportunity to introduce them to everyone we've met in the village.

"Okay, I guess I don't get the point of the case needing a party," I reply hesitantly.

"If the case isn't solved by Friday, then you and Quinn can talk to individual people and do an informal questioning under the guise of a friendly little party. You know, people will be relaxed and could let their guard down. If the case is solved, then it's an opportunity for people to get together for some fun."

"I guess. Let me make sure that it's fine with Quinn and that he can make it."

Karen beams at me, "I'm going ahead with the party. I think it will be fun!"

"Why'd you ask me about the party if you're going to do it anyway?"

"I didn't *ask* you about a party. I said what this case *needs* is a party."

I call Quinn and he tells me he's free that Friday night and would be interested in coming to the party.

Karen looks at me over the laptop. "When I'm done with the invitation, we'll need to find somewhere to print them out.

How many do you think we need? Who *are* we inviting anyway?"

"Well, let me see. Quinn, Fi, the O'Neil's, the Flynns, Fr. Kennedy, Maeve, Kathleen, Tom, Ralph, Tim, Claire and Harvey Clarke, Eric and Megan, us for sure. I may add a few others. I'll have to think about it. Maybe twelve copies, just in case I add more people later." Karen wanders off to plan the menu.

"While you're planning, I need to leave for the station."

"Give me ten minutes to get ready and I'll walk into town with you. There are a few shops I'd like to look through. I'll walk home when I'm done and meet you here later."

Once in town, Karen kisses me good-bye as I head into the Garda station where I find Quinn. He looks up from stacks of papers, some pencil stubs, two used coffee cups on his desk, and waves me over. "I asked Fi to come in today. She said she'd be here at 10. Do you want a cup of coffee while we wait?"

Fi arrives on time, and she's shown into an interview room. Quinn asks if I can be present and Fi offers no objection. Her hands check the ever-present dangly earrings and then arrange a ruffle on her blouse.

Quinn leans his elbows on table, "Fi, can you think of anyone who would want to see Laird O'Connor dead?"

"I'm sure there is more than one scorned lover or angry spouse out there."

"Any idea of the names of those scorned lovers or angry spouses?"

Fi smirks, "There's a rumor that Laird O'Connor had an affair with Diedre Flynn about a year and a half ago and that Brian was jealous. In fact, Brian and Dee separated for a short time due to the affair."

If that's true, it looks bad for Brian. But Fi's smirk bothers me.

Quinn responds nonchalantly, "Yes, we've heard a lot of rumors. And we're investigating every one of them."

Fi's smile is gone. Her hands clench. She juts her chin toward Quinn, "What are you hearing?"

"You and Laird O'Connor were more than employer/ employee. Is that true?"

"Yes. We were friends and support for each other during difficult times in our lives. He was a mentor to me."

"Were you friends with privileges?" Quinn questions.

"Ask the questions you really want to ask," Fi states in a haughty tone.

"Rumor has it you and Laird O'Connor were currently involved in a sexual relationship."

Fi's not smirking but her mouth is twisting. "Yes, Laird O'Connor and I were involved, sexually."

A thin smile appears at Quinn's mouth, "At the party you appeared surprised by the Laird's announcement that he planned to marry Colleen Moore. Did you believe the Laird would propose to you?"

"Don't be silly. I heard rumors of the Laird's behaviors and I clearly understood our relationship was not exclusive. I had no delusions I'd be the next Lady O'Connor. I was just surprised that he planned to marry again at all. Laird O'Connor appeared content with his rogue bachelor status."

My belief is when people use the phase, 'Don't be silly,' it's because it's closer to the truth than people would like, so I chime in, "Rumor has it that the marriage to Ms. Moore had more to do with a financial deal than love. Were you privy to the state of Lord O'Connor's financial situation?"

Icily, Fi looks directly at me, "As an expert fact finder, you of all people should know not to listen to idle village gossip. Where'd you get your information, the Lamb and Ram Investment group? If the people sitting on the stools in the local pub worked harder at actually working and less at rumor mucking, they might have more money in their pockets. There's nothing wrong with Laird O'Connor's financial situation."

Quinn inquires, "How are you so sure?"

Fi shrugs her shoulders, "I know for a fact that a development firm is interested in buying a few acres on the far west side of Baile Manor for a luxury resort. The firm made their first visit to the Manor about two months ago. As Laird O'Connor's personal assistant, I was aware of the meetings. I know that the Laird was offered several hundreds of thousands of euros for one hundred acres and that he was in negotiation with the firm. The Laird would hardly have needed a marriage of convenience to save his precious estate." Fi's last remark drips with sarcasm.

"The Laird was willing to sell part of the estate?" Quinn questions.

"The loss of 100 acres would not even have been noticed. The estate has over 2000 acres. The Laird was considering selling the old tenant farmer cottages, which are nothing but a few ruined stone buildings. All they are is an eyesore. He considered it a winning situation. He makes money, and the development firm clears away the ruins."

I'm curious at Fi's certainty that there was a deal and ask, "How can you be so sure? There doesn't appear to be any rumors circulating in the village." I think back to Angry Farmer and wonder if that was part his tirade. Fi's comment that a one-hundred-acre loss from 2000 acres not being noticed is strange. In the Laird's case, it's a portion of his heritage. A man who could tell stories of the family exploits won't feel comfortable losing so much of his past.

Fi's lips twitch with amusement, "I heard it from the project manager of the investment firm. Laird O'Connor and the investment firm were working very hard to keep the plan quiet. The concern was that other land values in the area would quickly rise. The firm was considering buying adjacent land for a larger development."

Quinn interrupts her, "You're saying the project manager just happened to tell you the particulars of the deal. Why?"

"You would be surprised what men will tell you over 'pillow

talk.' *My* relationship with Laird O'Connor wasn't exclusive, either."

This was an unexpected twist. If Laird O'Connor had a financial backup plan, and Fi wasn't maintaining an exclusive relationship with the Laird in hopes to become Lady O'Connor, then who had motive for the crime? Fi's mouth is tucked into a smug smile. Quinn's voice is professionally flat, "I need the name, address, and phone number of the investment firm and especially the project manager to verify your story." Good cop.

"Asking him how good I am in bed?" Fi's eyebrows twist. "The answer is, very good. You should know." Laughing, Fi reaches in her purse and removes her phone, "Not a problem. The project manager's name is William Jones. I have all his information here and can send it you right now."

A few seconds later Quinn receives the information on his phone and informs Fi that she's free to go but not to leave the village without notifying him first. When Fi reaches the door, she turns and announces, "Now that you know about Will, I should add that he can alibi me the night of Laird O'Connor's death. He and I were together from the time I arrived home after the party until the next morning. Will is on a per diem and its more cost effective for him to stay with me when he's in town."

"You didn't bring him to the party. Why not?" Quinn asked in a noncommittal tone.

Fi's voice lifts in triumph. Her laugh is brittle. "No one else was to be knowin' of the offer. Laird O'Connor would have died if it'd become knowledge too soon. Oops, excuse the pun." She leaves the room on another smile.

We simultaneously puff out a breath. Quinn throws his pen on the table, runs his hand over his hair, and says, “If this checks out, we just lost one of our prime suspects. I’d have bet my retirement on her being guilty. You know the old saying, ‘Revenge has no fury like a woman scorned.’ I’ve some phone calls to make to follow up on this lead. Also, I’m planning to request Colleen Moore come in.”

Quinn doesn’t acknowledge Fi’s comment of ‘You should know.’ Maybe Quinn has a motive for not finding Fi guilty? I hate this part of police work: no one—no one—is exempt from scrutiny.

“I need to contact Michael O’Connor to see what he knows about this, to see if he had motive or an alibi,” Quinn adds.

As I sit in the silence, I am speechless. Like Quinn, I’d have believed Fi had a strong motive, jealousy. She also had means and opportunity: living in the village, she’d have known if Brian Flynn hid a set of keys in his car and that Brian was drunk most nights. If Fi’s remark about Dee and Lord O’Connor is correct, then we are back to Brian Flynn having motive and means. However, what would’ve brought Lord O’Connor out that morning right after his party and announcement of engagement? I doubt a jealous husband. Interviewing Colleen Moore is a good next step, and so is finding Michael O’Connor.

Quinn interrupts my thoughts, “I plan to re-interview Brian Flynn regarding Fi’s statement about Laird O’Connor and Diedre having had an affair. Also, I’m callin’ Diedre in for questioning.”

My thoughts start again. What if the adjacent landowners found out about the possible deal and were angry with Lord O’Connor for selling? What about that angry sheep farmer? Did Fi have someone else commit the murder for her while she had an airtight alibi? I finish my cup of coffee and head for home.

Quinn catches me as I reach the door, "Colleen Moore will come in for an interview tomorrow at 11 a.m."

As I walk home, I replay everything over and over. I'm so engrossed in thought that I actually walk past the cottage and need to turn around and come back. Karen is on the couch reading a book, "Hi. How'd it go?"

"Fine, I guess. It appears we ran into a dead end. I'm not sure what my next move will be."

"YOUR next move?" Karen snorts, "I thought this was Quinn's case."

"Umm, that's what I meant, I can't think of what'll Quinn's next move be, except to find Lord O'Connor's son Michael and interview Colleen Moore."

Karen laughs, "I knew what you meant."

"Okay, Okay. What are we doing for lunch?"

"I ate two hours ago at noon."

"Then what am I doing for lunch now?"

"There is sandwich meat and bread if you want to make yourself a sandwich."

I don't need to think about how to slap meat onto bread. I've eaten my lunch late too many times in my career. But the case . . . It feels just too pat that Fi has an alibi for the night of Lord O'Connor's death. My "coppy sense," tells me not to let it go. I suspect that with time and more digging, Fi's cool will show cracks. I just can't think of where to look for the evidence that would prove my point. I'm not even sure what my point is. Is Fi an angry murderer or a cold-hearted bitch?

I suddenly hear, "Daniel." I look up and Karen is laughing at me.

“What? I ask.

“You have eaten two sandwiches and are reaching to make a third. Are you truly that hungry or did you lose track of what you are doing?”

“Oh, really, two full sandwiches?”

“Yes! Put down the bread, Detective, and step away from the counter. Move along, there’s nothing to see here.”

“Ha ha. You’re doing cop jokes now.”

Karen laughs and suggests a bike ride.

“Yes, I need to do something physical. How far should we ride?”

“I don’t care. How about we explore the road to the south of town and turn around when we’re tired?”

“It sounds like a plan and on the way back, I’ll buy you dinner at the Lamb and Ram for being such a good sport.”

Karen laughs, “I love a man with a plan!”

Two hours later we stop at the Lamb and Ram. We lock up the bikes in front of the pub. Karen and I enter the pub, and I see Brian. He comes out from behind the bar, shakes my hand, and says, “I want to say I’m sorry for how I acted before. How’s the case goin’?”

“I’m not sure, but I believe that Quinn is doing a good job.”

Brian shakes his head, “I feel like all eyes are watching me. The stress of not knowing bothers me most. I still can’t remember that night.”

“No matter how it turns out, I think Quinn will be fair with you. He’s a good cop.”

“I know.” Brian nods, “I’ve seen him grow up here and know the kind of man he is.”

"On a lighter note, what do you recommend for dinner?"

"The meatloaf sandwich with mash potatoes is great." He replies.

Karen and I both order that. Karen heads outside to find a table. I wait at the bar for our drinks. Brian says, "I know many people in the village think I'm good fer nothin.' That all I do is drink while in the pub. What they don't know is that I have pride in what I do here. A mate of mine worked at the Gravity Bar at the top of the Guinness factory and he schooled me in the art of the perfect pint. I'll show you what I learned. First you take a clean, dry Guinness glass, put it at forty-five degrees angle to the nozzle. Then pull the handle forward towards you until the beers fills up three quarters of the ways on the glass."

I ask, "How do you know it's three quarters full?"

"It's where the harp on the glass is. The special part is that the glass needs to rest for two minutes. That allows the nitrogen and CO2 gasses to mix, creating the surge to rise, called 'Going back down for the black.'" After the two minutes of silence except for the background medley of the pub, Brian continues, "The glass is held straight this time. The handle is pushed back, not forward because then it doesn't have as much gas in it and it keeps the head. Fill to the proud of the rim, don't let it spill over."

As Brian puts the glass in front of me, he announces, "That is the perfect pint!"

I'm impressed.

"Slainte."

"I don't know what that means."

"It's Irish for cheers."

I hold up my glass, "Slainte."

I take my pint back to the table along with Karen's soda.

Karen leans into me, whispering, "He didn't do it!"

"Who didn't do what?"

Karen explains, "Brian didn't kill Laird O'Connor, on purpose or by accident. I just feel he didn't. I can't explain why I feel it."

"I agree. The problem is getting evidence to prove the fact he didn't. If it's true, someone has gone to a great length to involve him or throw suspicion on him by using his car. My question is why? Because it was convenient or to cause a problem for Brian or both?" We stop talking as Brian brings our dinner to us. The meatloaf sandwich is delicious. Karen and I decide to linger over Irish Bread Pudding. After dinner, we ride home on a beautiful autumn evening. I feel better than I have all day.

Chapter 12

I wake this morning to the sound of a steady, soothing Irish rain, but my mind is racing. I get up, shower, and dress. I'm sitting at the kitchen table with a third cup of coffee.

"Good morning," I say as Karen later wanders out of the bedroom, still in her pajamas and slippers.

"How long have you been up?"

"Since about 5 a.m. I couldn't sleep. Too much on my mind. I had an epiphany last night, and I need to clarify something with Quinn."

"Fine. I'll attend the Beautification Committee Meeting today."

"How about later I buy you lunch at O'Neil's?"

"Sure. What time?"

"Let's say noon?"

"I'll meet you at the station, so I don't end up sitting at the restaurant by myself. I can work on arrangements for our party. I'll finish up the flyers before I meet you. Go, get outta here. I'll see you at noon. I love you."

"I love you, too." I hug her tight.

When I arrive at the station, Quinn calls me into a side office where a man sits, his hands loosely clasped in front of him, his head slightly bent, as though he's studying the table, looking for something. He must be about 35 years old. When I enter the room, he stands up and I judge he is approximately 6' tall. His shoulders look steady under the tweed coat. The neatly trimmed blond hair and strong blue eyes remind me of someone, but I'm not sure who until Quinn introduces him.

"Dan, may I introduce Michael O'Connor, Laird Arthur O'Connor's son. This is Dan Novice, a retired detective from the States who is helping with the investigation of your father's death."

Michael O'Connor extends his hand. As I shake it, I'm struck that neither his hand nor his general appearance is that of a person "living on the streets as a beggar" as Maeve had told Karen.

Quinn indicates a chair for me and says, "We located Mr. O'Connor, or should I say Laird O'Connor, late yesterday and asked him to come in to discuss the situation."

Michael shakes his head in disbelief, "Laird O'Connor. That's something I didn't think I'd ever hear."

"We have a few questions for you." Quinn picks up his pen and opens his notebook, "What was your relationship with your father?"

Michael leans back and crosses his arms, "I didn't have a relationship with my father."

"What recent contact have you had with your father?" Quinn continues.

"Look, my parents had my life laid out for me. Law school and then home to run the estate. That's not the life I wanted. I was an angry addict. I left home to prove to my father I was a better man than he would ever be." Michael wipes a hand across his forehead and sighs, "I was going to be the next world-famous rock and roll sensation."

I had to ask, "Did you ever live on the street like a beggar?"

Michael's head pops up as if his face was slapped, "No, it was never that bad. I lived with friends and in a few flop houses, but that'd be all."

"I'm sorry to interrupt. Please go on."

Michael continues, "After several years I realized I didn't have the talent to be a performer, but I met a manager who convinced me to get clean and sober as well as consider studying law and working in the industry that way. He paid for me to go to law school, which I did. Now I'm a solicitor and work for a music company in Dublin. I guess my parents had better insight than I gave them credit for." He shrugs his shoulders.

Quinn asks, "Have you and your father spoken since you left home?"

Michael laughs, "No. I don't know who I was trying to hurt more, my father or me. Yes, I am aware that he had been unfaithful to my mother more than once, but she always took him back. I did go to my mother's funeral, but I stood out of sight, and when it was over I placed flowers on her grave. At that moment I felt there was nothing left for me in Ballyram. I haven't been back since."

I clear my throat, "You now inherit everything. That can be a strong motive."

"I inherit a debt-ridden estate. I hope my father has enough life insurance to bury him. My father preferred to spend his money in the here and now. He rarely planned for the future. I don't see that as a motive, besides my father's death is an accident. Isn't it?"

Quinn focuses on Michael, "We're not sure, but the evidence appears to lean towards intentional homicide." His shoulders slope.

"Who'd want to kill him? It wouldn't be me. If I were going to kill him, I'd have done it five years ago, when my mother died. At that time, I was convinced my father's behavior led to my mother's early death. I'm a few years older and hopefully wiser."

I have to ask, "Can you think of anyone who would want him dead?"

Michael flicks a glance to me and then returns to studying Quinn. "I can't say. I kept an eye on my father for many years, but always from a distance. I'm sure there's more than one scorned lover or angry spouse out there. My father didn't let marriage vows stop him, his or anyone else's."

Quinn asks, "Do you have an alibi for the early morning hours on the day of your father's death?"

Michael doesn't shift his position, but his eyes are focused on Quinn. The new Laird's body is steady, "Where I am most Saturday nights. A bar in Dublin called Derry's, until the early morning hours, and at least five other mates can vouch for my being there."

My gut feeling is that Michael has the anger it took to commit this crime, but not the desire. A former addict in a bar? Either he has achieved balance, or he has his demons under control. Looking at him, I'd put money on the second.

Quinn inquires, "Will you be staying in town or returning to Dublin?"

"I'll be staying in town at O'Neil's Bed and Breakfast because," he pauses, "the Manor holds no fond memories for me, and I'm sure there is much to sort out regarding the estate."

"Well, you have my sympathies. You're free to go. Don't be goin' back to Dublin without lettin' me know."

There's no formal good-bye. Michael O'Connor gets up slowly and walks out of Quinn's office.

After Michael leaves, Quinn turns to me, "What do you think?"

"My feeling is he didn't do it."

"I don't think so either."

Cocking my head to one side, "Do you think he's aware of the investment firm's offer to buy the land? If the development plan goes through, it'd mean Michael O'Connor isn't inheriting a debt-ridden estate."

"That thought crossed me mind. I'd like to do a bit of a check on his alibi. Now what?"

"I thought you had asked Colleen Moore in for an interview, but I don't see her."

"Ms. Moore informed me that she would not be available today due to a previous commitment. My first thought is she's lining up a high-priced solicitor before she'll agree to an interview. I ordered her in tomorrow. You available?"

Guilt flashes through my mind and then vivid images of my wife, followed by a surge of professional curiosity. "Yes. I'll be very interested to see what Ms. Moore has to say. First, I'll have to be sure Karen and I don't have plans. Karen wants me to remind you of the party on Friday."

"I've made a note of it in me calendar. I've Diedre in an interview room. Care to join me?"

Quinn and I enter the interview room. Diedre is pale, with the crust of tear tracks on her face. Two of the blouse buttons are in the wrong holes and her sweater hangs crooked.

Quinn starts softly, "Thank you for coming in. I know this is hard, but you lied to us about where Brian was the night of Laird O'Connor's death, and I need to know about your relationship with Laird O'Connor."

Diedre shakes her head.

"Diedre, remember that we're recording, and the tape cannot show you shaking your head. Did you have an intimate relationship with Laird O'Connor?"

"NO! When Brian and me separated, I took a job as cook at the Manor. It was a very bad time for me. His Lairdship be very kind. Many times, he would come into me kitchen in the wee hours of the mornin' and we'd talk. Just talk. I think he was a bit sad and lonely."

"I'm sorry, Dee, but I've to ask: did you and his Lairdship have a physically intimate relationship?"

"NO, I told ya! He tried his charm on me and I think he was willin', but I weren't. I knew his ways. I love my husband. When Brian promised to get capped, I went back home. That was the end of me 'relationship' with his Lairdship, except passin' in the village, not that it stopped the gossip."

I look at Quinn quizzically, "I don't know what the expression 'get capped' means."

Quinn replies, "Sorry. 'Get capped' is an Irish saying that means a person needs to start thinkin' straight. Deidre, what about Brian? Could he have done this some night while he was drinkin?"

Her blue eyes are electric with anger, solely focused on Quinn, "No. Brian's a good man. He's got himself a good heart. He wouldn't be goin' out running over people with his car and then just be leavin them."

Diedre drops her head. Her body quivers as she begins sobbing.

Quinn and I exchange glances. Quinn shakes his head, "You're free to go for now. I may be havin' more questions for you later." Diedre shuffles out as if sleepwalking through this nightmare that is now her life.

Quinn and I discuss our next step when I look at my watch. I excuse myself to meet Karen in the lobby. It's a short walk to O'Neil's Bed and Breakfast. Nora greets us and shows us to a table. We read over the menu and decide on a hamburger and a cheeseburger.

Karen tells me, "The invitations for our party are done. I've decided on a theme of 'World Tourism Day.' I was searching for a fun theme for the party when I came across this website that lists a holiday for each day of the year. September 27 is 'World Tourism Day.' I thought it would be interesting to combine foods from the U.S. and Ireland."

"What is World Tourism Day?"

"I did some internet research and, I quote, 'Since 1980, the United Nations World Tourism Organization has celebrated World Tourism Day on September 27. The purpose of this day is to raise awareness on the role of tourism within the international community and to demonstrate how it affects social, cultural, political and economic values worldwide.'"

"It sounds like a great idea."

Karen tells Nora that she would love dessert but is full. I offer to eat any dessert she doesn't finish, so Karen orders Very Fruity pie with ice cream.

Sean lays the plate in front of Karen, "That recipe is me

wife's very own creation and I dare ya to be learnin' her 'secret' ingredient. No one has been able to figure it out. I'll give ya a hint, it is fruit and it's rare. That's all I'll be sayin' on the subject." He winks before heading back into the kitchen.

He's gone before Karen says, "I'll take that challenge and I bet I win. It appears I'll have some extra time on my hands to work on it as you seem determined to see this investigation to its conclusion."

I nod affirmatively.

"I see raspberries, blackberries, blueberries, but there is a favor I can't place. It's not strawberries or orange. When we get back to the cottage, I'll do some research on the Internet to see if there are any hints. I hope you're hungry for pie because you may be eating several attempts before I learn her 'secret.'"

A smile creases my face, "I love pie."

I wonder how many experimental pies I'll have to eat. We finish up and say our good-byes to Nora and Sean as we walk back to the cottage.

On the way home I tell Karen, "Hey, I bumped into Fr. Kennedy on my way to the station this morning. He asked how we liked the village so far. One thing led to another and we started talking about the village and its history, as well as of St. Patrick's church. Anyway, Fr. Kennedy has offered to give us a tour of both the church and the cemetery."

"That sounds great. And I have news from the Beautification Meeting. I think Maeve is in love with Tim Clarke. She practically sighs when he makes a suggestion and expects everyone to support the idea. She demands quiet from the others whenever he speaks."

"It might be nice for Tim to have someone, again," I say.

"Also, I noticed Kathleen seemed very happy and I commented on it. She said it's sad that Laird O'Connor is dead, but he personally was causing her a great deal of stress and now the stress is gone."

"What?" I lean forward.

"Apparently there were some stone ruins on Laird O'Connor's estate and he planned to sell the land, which means the ruins would be removed by a developer."

"Okay, why was Kathleen stressed about it?"

"Because that's where her fairies live and where she goes there to meet them. She also believes that Laird O'Connor's plan to destroy the ruins is the reason that he died."

"Seriously? She believes a fairy's curse killed him!"

"She understands that a person killed him, but she thinks the murderer may have been under the fairy's control."

"Okay, but my experience has been that there's more evil in real people than all magic combined."

"I understand, but Kathleen is very sensitive when it comes to *her* fairies and their well-being. I'm just relaying what she said."

"Well, it could be a novel defense. The fairies controlled my mind and made me do it," I laugh.

"Don't be mean!" Karen frowns and her eyes flash with anger.

"You're right. I'm sorry. Maybe Kathleen was possessed by the fairies and felt as if she had to act to save them, a form of self-defense. I just wonder if Quinn and I should have a talk with Kathleen as to the extent she would go to protect her fairies and their home."

Karen states, "Before the meeting, Oona O'Leary and I talked about whether or not it would be possible for us to bring Hannah up to see the sheep when the kids come for a visit. I apologized for upsetting her husband the other day. Well, Oona said that her husband has always had a temper, but recently he had a stroke and has limited use of his left side. The couple's youngest son is helping run the farm, but her husband is never happy with his work. Charles wants his eldest son to run the farm, but that son has his own farm and family. Oona is worried about her husband because she believes he's depressed, but he won't see anyone about it. She knows her husband is cranky, but she said she'd find a time for us to visit when he's gone."

"That's very nice of her as long as she's sure it won't cause a problem with her husband," I say skeptically.

"I almost forgot. Oona mentioned in passing that her husband was out drinking at the Lamb and Ram the night Laird O'Connor was killed. She said she received a call from someone at the pub, informing her that Charles was very angry and talking nonsense."

My head snaps up, now I'm curious, "Did she say what her husband was saying?"

"Yes. Apparently, he said that rich people feel they can stomp on anyone they choose. He ranted that the rich just feel they can take what they want. And he said they need to be stopped permanently. Oona went down to the pub and was able the convince him to come home."

"Did she say what time she got him home?"

"She said about 1:30 in the morning, but that's not the interesting part. She woke up an hour or so later to find Charles wasn't in bed nor could she find him in the house."

"Did she ask him where he was?"

"Yeah. He told her he went for a drive, which she said didn't make sense. Driving at night has been a problem for him since the stroke, but she didn't want to push for further details because he gets so angry."

"It appears the list of possible suspects is growing."

A smile creeps across Karen's face, "Yes, it would appear so."

"The sad part is that Oona is afraid they might lose the farm because of her husband's disability and the growing tension between Charles and their son. Apparently, their son is threatening to leave and take a job he was offered as Estate Manager for guess who?"

"Not Laird O'Connor."

"Exactly!"

"That's a motive." My mind is calculating. If O'Connor is dead, the O'Leary son can't leave a farm to be estate manager. But the O'Leary son would still be around and be financially able to help his parents. Then again, what would a Laird in financial straits be able to pay an estate manager?

Karen's voice interrupts my speculations, "And Charles blames Brian Flynn for calling Oona to come and pick him up at the pub."

"I'll give Quinn all of this information and he can follow up on it."

"Well played, Detective."

Chapter 13

I wake up to rain outside again today. Irish weather in autumn can be this way, but we've been very lucky in avoiding it most days. The trip into town will be wet and sloppy, and I remind myself I'm retired. I don't have to go out in this weather, but my curiosity won't allow 'a wee bit' of rain from stopping me. A voice behind me says, "It looks like you're going to get wet on your way to the station today."

"I was just thinking about whether or not to go in today."

Karen sighs, "You won't be much company today with your thoughts on what's being said in the interviews. Go talk everything out with Quinn.

I laugh, "Deal!"

I get to the police station as Colleen Moore arrives accompanied by a tall and overly thin man, bending toward her, whispering. He looks like a whippet with a bad case of mange. She is truly a beautiful woman, wearing blue and grey. I follow behind as they're shown into an interview room. Before he closes the interview room door, Quinn nods his head toward a second door. I watch from a viewing room, settling myself on the front edge of the dented folding chair and peering forward into the interview room.

Ms. Moore is sitting straight-backed on one of the chairs. Her hands are folded in her lap and her shoulders are rigid. Her eyes flick with rage and her jaw is set. Her attorney introduces himself,

"I'm James Moore, Ms. Moore's cousin. I'm with the Dublin law firm of O'Brien and Brady."

James Moore is wearing a perfectly tailored grey flannel, pinstriped suit. His black leather shoes are buffed to a high shine. He presents Quinn with a business card held out between two fingers.

Mr. Moore opens the conversation, "Why are we here?"

"Because Ms. Moore was close to a victim in a murder investigation, she was present in the victim's home on the night of the incident, and I'm interested in what she knows about the situation."

"Are you implying she had something to do with the accident?"

"Did she?"

"No, she did not."

Quinn turns his shoulder toward the attorney and faces Ms. Moore, "Do you know anyone who would have reason to want Laird O'Connor dead?"

"I thought it was an accident. Are you calling it murder now?" Colleen asks.

Coolly, Quinn replies, "We're exploring all avenues."

Colleen's answer is icy cold with each word cut off and presented separately, "My first thought would be that Lynch woman. She has been trying to position herself as the next Lady O'Connor for years and was quite upset at Arthur's announcement of our engagement."

"Who told you that?" Quinn asks.

"No one had to tell me. I heard it for myself. The night of the party after Arthur and I thought everyone had left, I went to the kitchen when Fionnuala Lynch stepped out of the library and confronted Arthur. She was crying and yelling about feeling used and betrayed. She also asked how Arthur could do that to her after all they had meant to each other." Colleen waves a hand dismissively, "Arthur tried to explain that he never intended her to be anything but a distraction and that their relationship wasn't exclusive. Arthur asked her to leave, but she held onto his arm, crying and begging him to reconsider. Arthur walked her to the door and practically pushed her out. But even then, she pounded on the door. She kept saying that Arthur would be sorry, and it was a big mistake."

"What happened next?"

"Arthur and I went to bed. I took a sleeping pill, but I think his mobile rang during the night. All I know is when I woke up in the morning he wasn't in bed. I assumed he woke up early and went downstairs for breakfast. I got up and went to look for him, but none of the servants had seen him."

My coppy sense is asking why she had to take a sleeping pill on the night her engagement to the handsome and eligible Laird was announced.

"What time was this?"

"Maybe 7 a.m."

"Then what did you do?"

"I assumed he went for a walk, so I went back to bed until you showed up to tell me about the accident."

"You've no idea who would've called or what time the call came in?"

"I'm not sure there was a call. I told you, I had taken a sleeping pill."

"Can you think of anyone else with a motive to kill Laird

O'Connor besides Fi Lynch?" Quinn presses.

"Well, I've heard Arthur was killed by a car belonging to the idiot from the Lamb and the Ram. Arthur had mentioned more than once that Flynn guy killed his best friend but kept on drink and driving around town. He also said he was surprised that Flynn hasn't killed someone else. Well, maybe now he has. Have you interviewed that guy?"

Quinn nods and flatly states, "We are interviewing everyone possibly associated with the situation. Back to Laird O'Connor, can you think of anyone else with a grudge against him?"

"Rumors of jealous ex-lovers and/or spouses, but nothing Arthur ever mentioned to me. He didn't 'kiss and tell.' Am I free to go?"

Mr. Moore stands up and extends his hand; his cousin gracefully rises out of her chair and places her hand in his.

At Quinn's words, he freezes, "My concern is that you don't have an alibi for the time of Laird O'Connor's death. Is there anyone who can vouch that you didn't leave the manor that night?"

Mr. Moore turns his attention from his cousin to the officer and says, "My client has answered your questions to the best of her knowledge. I feel you're on a 'fishing expedition' now. Either charge my client or we're leaving. Make a decision."

Quinn has no option. He does caution her to remain available for further questioning, if needed. To which Ms. Moore replies, "Speak to my attorney in the future." She stands, her coat moving around her as regally as a robe of state. Ms. Moore and her cousin leave, neither of them looking at Quinn as they pass him.

When I join Quinn in the interview room, he asks, "What do you think of Ms. Moore?"

"She's tough. If she did it, she isn't giving in easily. I'm having a hard time reading her, but I don't think she did it. At the party Laird O'Connor and Ms. Moore appeared happy, so I find it hard to believe the relationship dissolved so quickly and terribly within a matter of hours to leave one of them dead."

"Brian Flynn is in another interview room. Care to help with the interview?"

"I wouldn't miss it."

Quinn and I enter the interview room. Brian appears visibly shaken. Quinn begins, "Brian, during the course of the investigation we've heard certain rumors including that Laird O'Connor had an affair with your wife. First I need to know if it's true or not?"

Brian is defiant, "No, Deidre would never!" His hands clench and spasm. He looks from Quinn to me.

"Well, the other rumor was that you and Deidre separated for a period of time about a year or so ago. Is that true?"

"It's true, but not because she had an affair. Dee went to her mother's house because of my drinking. I was angry with her and found meself drinking more and more and trying to act as if I was single. You know, no wife to answer to. One morning I find meself in bed with Fionnuala Lynch. I have no memory of what had happened, but I knew I made a terrible mistake. Fionnuala started talking about how she had always fancied us a couple and now we could be. I tried to reason with her and tell her whatever happened was just a terrible mistake. We couldn't have a relationship because I was still in love with Dee. Fi was so angry she threatened to tell Dee."

"Did you tell Dee?"

"I was afraid Dee would leave for good. I couldn't be sure who had seen me and Fi together. Fi promised to keep her mouth shut," he paused and stared at the ceiling, "for a price. She started blackmailing me." Brian's face reddens, "I'm such a coward." Tears slide from the corners of his eyes and mesh with the snot from his nose. I hate it when guys cry. But he's had a hard time.

"Brian, I have it on good authority that you and Fi had an argument on Friday, September 6."

"I received a call from Fi. I'm not sure which day. She wanted to meet to discuss the 'situation.' I told her I wanted it to stop. She laughed at me and said that no one uses her and then throws her aside. She threatened to tell Dee and everyone in town, includin' me parents. I couldn't stand the embarrassment to my family, so I backed down and paid her. There were times she would come into the pub just to push me buttons. Often Fi would make remarks in front of Dee that suggested Fi and I had an ongoing relationship. Dee asked about the comments once or twice, but I denied everything."

"How did the rumors get started about Dee and Laird O'Connor?"

Brian's body snaps forward as he spats out, "Me money would be on Fi starting the rumors. That's just the way she is. I had no quarrel with Laird O'Connor and no reason for wanting him dead."

Quinn and I sigh in unison. The question I'm sure we are both thinking is *where do we go from here?* Quinn releases Brian with advice to have an honest conversation with Deidre before she hears the truth from someone else, like Fi. Brian's head is hanging low, like a beaten man, and he slowly shuffles out of the station.

Quinn informs me that he followed up on Fionnoula's alibi with William Jones, and the project manager confirms that Fi was with him at the time of Laird O'Connor's death. Mr. Jones stated that he was in town for the weekend to finish the surveying. He confirms that he was at Fi's place when she arrived home from the party at approximately 12:30 a.m. and they were together the rest of the night. Mr. Jones reports that he and Fi woke up together and had breakfast at her place on Sunday morning. He left around 10 a.m. to drive back to Dublin. Quinn is exasperated, "I don't know where to go from here."

"Could Fi have left the house without him knowing it?"

"Mr. Jones was adamant that she didn't."

I shake my head from side to side, debating on how to say this without sounding crazy. I decide to just say it, "I've learned that a couple other people may have had a motive. The first is Kathleen Kelly. Karen overheard her threating Laird O'Connor because the land he was selling to the developer was where her fairies reside. I believe her quote was, 'You can't let this happen. If you don't do something, I will.'" I swear the faintest trace of a smile twitched on Quinn's lips. I continue, "And Charles O'Leary was out of the house the night of the murder. He was heard threatening Laird O'Connor and got angry with Brian for calling his wife to pick him up from the Lamb and Ram."

Quinn nods, "I'll question them both."

As the case races through my head, I decide to go home for now.

I open the front door to the scent of homemade pie. Karen is in the kitchen. It feels warm and comfy. "Hello. I'm home."

"I'm trying to recreate Mrs. O'Brien's Fruity Pie. I found a mixed fruit pie recipe online and am trying my own variation. I added some of the juice from a jar of maraschino cherries. Also, I added brown sugar in addition to the white sugar the recipe called for. I think it's cool enough for a taste test.

I cut myself a generous slice, take a bite and stop. Karen is intensely watching me, and then says, "What do you think?"

"I'm sorry, not even close. It's very sweet and has a different taste completely." My teeth hurt from all that extra sugar.

"Maybe next time I won't add the additional brown sugar. Mrs. O'Brien must add something that intensifies the flavor. I wonder if Mr. Doyle at the grocery store will reveal her 'secret' ingredient."

I laugh, "So YOU intend to do some detective work while professing to be retired, huh?"

Karen laughs, "You have a point." She takes a slice of pie.

"Do you like it that sweet?"

"Please, it has sugar. Of course, I like! You have beer, I have sweets," Karen replies.

Chapter 14

At 9 a.m. Karen and I arrive for our prearranged tour with Father Kennedy. The skin under his eyes is puffy and black. He appears to carry the worries of his parishioners on his face. He's waiting for us in front of the two massive oak doors trimmed with ornate metal screws and hinges that form the entrance to the church. The planks that combine to form the front door are wide and weathered. The church is constructed of the same field stone that form the walls of the fields I pass along the roadway to Ballyram: grey and tan with bits of moss clinging to a number of the stones.

"Bueno Dias, Padre," I laugh, shaking his hand

"Maidin Mhaith," Fr. Kennedy replies, "That's Irish for 'Good morning.'"

When Fr. Kennedy opens the door, it creaks with age. We cross the threshold into the echoes and drop our voices.

Fr. Kennedy begins, "St Patrick's Church was built on the site of the old Chapel of the Holy Cross. The church was consecrated on St. Patrick's Day in 1865. But its history is much older."

It's dim inside, even on a sunny day, and smells of cold stone, ancient wood, and old people. It feels dry inside even with the moisture that descends on Ireland.

"The altar is made of Carrara marble and was erected in 1919 to replace the original wooden altar. The devotion to Ireland is evident in the three front stained-glass windows." Father Kennedy points to each one as he speaks, "One is a portrait of our Lord and Savior, Jesus Christ; one our patron saint, St. Patrick himself; and one the symbol of the church, three-leaf clover. The Father, the Son, and the Holy Spirit."

To me, the altar looks like a heavy, damp, grey stone.

We follow Fr. Kennedy out a tiny door in the robing room, and step into the sunlit graveyard where there are tipped headstones with wind worn names, green grass leaning with the breeze, the smell of dirt, and the sound of sobbing.

Mr. Clarke kneels before a head stone, tears flowing, unaware that we are there.

Fr. Kennedy drops his voice, "Nothing here that mankind can help with, only God can give peace. It's a tragic story. Mr. Clarke's only son, Patrick, was killed in an auto accident four years ago and his daughter, Miora, less than two years ago. His wife passed shortly after Moira, I fear of a broken heart. He's here every week, praise his devotion." Sadness creeps into Father Kennedy's voice, "Some wounds never heal, especially when the other person in the car walks away without a scratch. I normally leave him to himself but remain available if he chooses. As said in Deuteronomy, 'It is mine to avenge; I will repay. In due time their foot will slip; their day of disaster is near and their doom rushes upon them.'"

Some wounds never heal? Fr. Kennedy has more inside him than I thought.

I think back to Tim's words at the accident scene. "Not only is he sad, but there is also a great deal of anger. Has he spoken to you about it?" I ask.

"It is not my place to say. Let's continue with our tour." Father Kennedy turns and walks back toward the church. We follow him back inside. He continues with various rooms inside and their functions, but I'm not listening. My mind continues to think over Mr. Clarke's situation and if there is any connection to what has happened recently. Karen is saying, "Thank you, Father. This was wonderful. We appreciate you giving us your time."

I automatically extend my hand and shake Father Kennedy's as I mumble, "Thank you and good-bye."

He heads toward the church then turns back towards us, "I was walking past the constabulary the other day and saw a little green sports car. I've learned that it belongs to Michael O'Connor. I thought I should mention it."

I laugh, "Mercedes Benz SL Roadster. Being a lawyer can do that for you."

"No, it's not the car that's important. It's that fact that I saw the car driving through town the day of Laird O'Connor's party at approximately 3 p.m. I remember because it's such a unique car."

I think back to the interview Quinn and I had with Michael, who clearly indicated that he had not been back to Ballyram since college, except for his mother's funeral.

Once back at the cottage, I phone Quinn to inform him I have 'an anonymous source' placing Michael O'Connor back in Ballyram prior to the date Michael first told us."

Justice works fast in Ballyram. An hour later, Quinn, Michael O'Connor, and I are sitting in a station interview room. Quinn starts, "Mr. O'Connor, we have an eyewitness that places you in Ballyram on the day before your father's death. That is well before when you stated you first returned to Ballyram since leaving all those years ago. Why the lie?"

"Not so much a lie . . . as a . . . delaying technique."

"Delaying technique? Delaying what?"

"Becoming the prime suspect. If you knew I was in Ballyram shortly before my father was killed, I'd head to the top of the suspect list. I was hoping with the additional time you would find the real perpetrator and I wouldn't need to explain my presence in Ballyram."

Quinn asks, "Do you know anything about his death?"

"No, but it didn't make sense that my father would have a grand party and suddenly feel the need for a walk down an unlit road at some insane time in the early morning. When I heard the report of his death, the first thought was that 'accident' made no sense."

"Why were you in Ballyram on Saturday?"

"I learned of his plans to sell off part of the estate from mutual friends in Dublin. I was angry that my father would sell the family heritage."

I interject, "You said you didn't care about the estate"

Michael's eyes flash with anger, "Yes, that's what I said when you were looking for a suspect, but it's still my family home and has been for generations. My father should have worked hard to keep it, but he was one to always take the easy way out of a problem. I had a meeting with him to let him know how I felt."

"Were you angry enough to threaten to stop him?" Quinn questions.

Michael's tone is cold, "No. When I confronted me father, it felt like the same old fight from years ago. I was expecting better from him, but he talked to me as if I were a child. I knew nothing had changed and nothing would, so I left. But I never raised a hand toward him."

Quinn continues, "So, where were you at the time of your father's death?"

"Well, depending on the exact time, as I told you earlier, I was either sitting in a Dublin pub named Derry's getting royally drunk until closing or passed out in my flat above the pub."

"When did you learn of your father's death?"

"The next morning around 7 a.m., I received a phone call from a friend in the village informing me of my father's untimely passing."

"Who's the friend?"

"I'd rather not say." Michael looks directly at Quinn, "I'd nothing to do with the murder, and I knew that sooner or later you'd find me in Dublin because I wasn't hiding. Do you have any more questions? If not, then I'm leaving."

Quinn shakes his head from side to side and opens his mouth to speak, when Michael holds up his hand and says, "Okay, I know what you're going to say, 'You're free to go for now, but don't leave town' or something to that effect. I'm a lawyer and know how this works."

Quinn looks after Michael as he's leaving and asks, "What do ya say about liking him for the murder?"

"I still don't think he did it," I rub my chin, "unless he had an accomplice."

Quinn nods in agreement. "I think a check of Michael's phone records may prove interesting. I'll start working on the warrant to open his phone records for cell, home, and work. I'm curious to find out who his 'friend' is."

"How did this 'friend' know at 7 a.m. that it was Laird O'Connor who was dead? You and I has only found out ourselves that the Laird was the victim."

Karen and I had talked this morning about meeting for lunch at Foley's, the other pub in town. I don't want to appear as if I am not impartial. We were supposed to meet at noon, but now it's going to be a late lunch. The pub is packed. The smell of warm bodies and fresh beer assault my nose. I use my body to maneuver through the crowd and find a small table at the far end of the room.

"Ah! You're here to watch the Hurling on the telly!" an elderly gentleman toasts us. "We shall win! The boys'll do us proud!"

The only 'hurling' I've encountered is projectile vomiting, but mindful of my mouth, I nod. Then I remember Hurling is the National sport of Ireland. Men stand at the bar, stand shoulder to shoulder, and almost stand on the chairs. They shout, they toast the screen, and then comment to their friends about the plays, last week's plays, last season's plays. It's louder than any football game. My ears ring.

"I don't think we're going to see menus. Not with it being this busy. Order two different things for dinner. I'm sure it will be fine," Karen shouts to me. I again work my way through the crowd, this time to make it to the bar. At the end of the bar, in a corner where the T.V.'s volume is softer but the surrounding cheers just as loud, I notice two people who are not following the game. A thin man dressed in a Garda uniform leans over the bar to talk to Michael Foley; I sidle behind him. The program switches to a commercial, the drinkers bury their chins in their beers, and there are a few seconds of relative quiet. Even though he lowered his voice, I can hear.

"Quinn is in charge because he's young and if he solves the murder, administration will take credit for it." The Garda officer quickly looks over both his shoulders, "But if Quinn screws it up, administration will dismiss Quinn as a way to appease new Laird O'Connor and the villagers. The new 'favorite' sergeant will be history in the village." Both men laugh.

I take two steps back, ducking behind a few patrons. A moment later I step forward to where Michael can see me. He looks embarrassed and wary, but I put on my best poker face and pretend I didn't hear anything.

"Dan! Good to see you know the best place to find food! This is me Uncle Shawn, the best sergeant with the Garda. Knows everything."

With a smile on my face, I extend my hand. I'm more determined to help Quinn any way I can with this investigation.

"Didja see that!" The yelling has started up again, so I lean over the bar to shout my order to Michael. He nods, taps me a Guinness and a diet coke for Karen, and walks to the kitchen to put in the food order.

Sgt. Foley stares at me for a few seconds, "I see you've sense drinkin' in the better pub. Too bad Quinn isn't as wise. People in this village know what happens when you're mates with Brian Flynn." A smirk crosses Sgt. Foley's face, "A mate could end up dead. Quinn still believes in Flynn. How you comin' along with investigation? I'd be the lead investigator on this case, but with my retiring, the brass decided to give it their 'wonder boy.' They put a lot of hope in him. I know that young Quinn is leaning on you a lot."

Twice in two minutes? He must think Americans are dense. I

refuse to break eye contact, choke down my ire, and reply, "Not as much as you think. Quinn is sharp and has a good quantitative mind." I hope Sgt. Foley is puzzled by what I mean. So much for the poker face. It's the words that count here.

Michael's at his uncle's side and says, "I'm happy to see ya willing to give Foley's a second chance. Thank you kindly. I promise you won't be disappointed."

I nod politely. The yelling is deafening as Ireland scores and the crowd gets louder. Karen and I cheer along with the other pub patrons. I look across the room and see Maeve and Kathleen at another table. Maeve gives me an emphatic nod of approval.

Back at the table I lean into to Karen and whisper, "Don't look now, but Maeve and Kathleen are here, and it appears that Maeve approves of our choices in pubs."

Michael signals that our food is ready. When I reach the bar, Maeve is there ordering another pint. Michael has moved to the other end of the bar to wait on other patrons.

Maeve shouts, "I see you've decided to drink at the better pub. Brilliant."

"I haven't decided anything. I've no issues with anything or anyone in the village."

Maeve's face wrinkles, "Well, I *know* for sure this is not the first time Brian killed someone with a car after drinking and got away with it. You'd never find me in his pub!"

Such a nice little old lady with such firm opinions, I tell myself. Possibly a little potted, too. Maeve sways as she lifts the pint to her mouth: more than a little potted.

I weave back to the table, where Karen and I dig in. Karen has a hamburger and I have a cheeseburger. Both are better than the fish and chips we had before. Ireland wins and the celebration begins. Karen and I each have another round of drinks before heading home. As we walk, I fill Karen in on what Maeve said to me. I wait until we're home before I inform Karen about what I overheard Sgt. Foley saying.

"Are you sure you heard him correctly? It was pretty loud in the pub," Karen asks.

"I'm sure. It pisses me off when I hear things like that about good, young cops."

Karen laughs, crossing her arms across her chest, "You went to the bar for our drinks, but you ended up playing spy."

"Just so you know I'm already resolved to help him any way I can."

Karen suggests a bike ride and we spend a couple hours on a ride. Karen heads off for a nap and I settle in with a book.

I had invited Quinn for dinner. He arrives at 6 p.m. Karen has made chicken breasts stuffed with a combination of wild rice and broccoli, along with steamed peas. Talk is light, Quinn raves about the dinner. It's followed by Karen's second attempt at Mary's pie recreation. It's not as sweet, but still not correct.

I steer the conversation toward what Karen and I learned today, "Tell me more about the case involving Brian and Tim's son."

Quinn smiles, "A little over four years ago, I was new to the force and the accident was the talk of the village. Gossip and speculation were everywhere."

"What happened?"

"The truth is only one person knows for sure. Brian Flynn and Paddy Clarke were best mates since childhood. Two peas in a pod, as me mum would say. More like nitro and glycerin, if you ask me. Alone they were fine, but together, nothin' but problems."

"So, what happened the day that Patrick was killed?"

"Paddy and Brian had been out drinking all day. Several people placed them at both the pubs in town. Later that night they hit a tree and Paddy was killed."

Karen gasps, "Oh, that's horrible."

I turn on investigation mode, "So, who was driving? Paddy or Brian?"

"That's the problem. When the police arrived at the scene, Brian was out of the car, both front car doors were open, and Paddy was on the ground near the driver's side. He was dead at the scene."

"Why the mystery? What didn't add up at the scene?"

"Sgt. Foley was the first to arrive. He reported that the driver's seat was pushed all the way back. Brian's more than a head taller than Paddy. Brian said that the seat must have slammed back when the car hit the tree. Both men smelled of alcohol, but Brian walked away with a few bruises, nothing more. Rumor was that Paddy's body had been moved, but Brian made the statement that he pulled Paddy out to provide aid. The biggest problem was that there was no way to prove who was driving."

Shaking my head and my finger for emphasis, "That's not true. My experience in accident reconstruction is that in a head-on collision the seat moves forward, not back."

"No eye witnesses, just Brian's word for what happened. So, Foley's official report was that the accident was Paddy's fault and nothin' more was investigated. Paddy's pa protested, but it never went any further. He resents Brian and to a certain degree, Foley, even to this day."

Karen agrees, "How would you get over losing a child, whether or not it's their fault especially if the other person just walked away. That would break my heart forever."

"Yeah, it really divided the village. People either supported Brian or vilified him. The pub where people drink determines which side a person is on. Supporters drink at the Lamb and Ram, others drink at Foley's.

"Being new to the village, I drink at both. I'm not sure which way I lean just yet."

"I just like me a pint now and again. It doesn't matter where it's from." Quinn nods affirmatively, "I work for everyone in the village."

Karen breaks in, "This is one of the saddest things I've heard. It's not what happens, it's how people deal with what happens. Who wants to hang onto anger and unhappiness? What would they gain from it?"

Quinn says, "It's still an open case. It's one of the cases I'd like to revisit as an exercise for this upcoming exam."

I feel myself being excited at the thought of helping Quinn work on two cases, one new and one old.

Quinn breaks my thoughts, "I interviewed Kathleen. I thought it best to speak to her alone. I asked her about her theory about the fairies and the threat of harm to anyone distrubin' their home."

Leaning forward, I ask "What'd she say?"

"Mostly she cried. Well, sobbed is a better description. She kept repeating how important the fairies are to Ireland and that their feelings are important too. She couldn't look at me. She was an emotional mess. I just can't see her as cold-hearted criminal. Someone who steals another person's car, hits the Laird and then backs over them while he's on the ground. I won't eliminate her completely, but she isn't the prime suspect."

"I think she really has a kind heart and wants what's best for people and the village." Karen adds.

"Me mum agrees with you. She found out about my questioning Kathleen, and I got an earful from her. She kept goin' on about how Kathleen is a gentle soul, and I was wrong to think Kathleen could have anything to do with the Laird's death. Me mum was more than a little upset with me." Quinn rolls his eyes.

Quinn and I set up some time to meet and he bids us good night. Karen and I clean up and head off to bed, but the image of Mr. Clarke at the cemetery is printed on the view screen in my mind. Resentment is a strong emotion and with time, it can grow. I wonder if it has grown to the point of taking revenge. This case has more questions than answers. What's my next step?

Chapter 15

The next day, I catch up with Quinn at the station, and he offers, "We're back to our list of suspects. I ran a background check on Colleen Moore. It appears she has a bit of a temper. She was charged with Attempted Murder. The complaint states that approximately five years ago Ms. Moore tried to kill her husband because she learned he was having an affair with his private secretary."

My eyebrows rise, "Apparently, she doesn't like men who cheat on her. So, it seems strange that she would settle on the Laird, who came with a reputation."

Quinn snorts, "The interesting part is Ms. Moore tried running over her husband with her car. He ended up with a broken leg."

"What happened to the case?"

"She ended up pleading to a greatly reduced charge because he refused to press charges. Apparently, he stated that it was just a 'misunderstanding.' Ms. Moore paid a small fine and that was the end of it. They divorced shortly after that."

To me that sounds as if she has political connections, considering how a small fine wouldn't even be noticeable to someone with Ms. Moore's money. I shift in my seat, "Laird O'Connor had a reputation for playing the field even during his marriage. Do you think Ms. Moore found out he was still 'active' and decided that she wasn't gonna to tolerate it?"

"But if she wanted to be Lady O'Connor, why not wait until

after they were married?" Quinn asks.

"I don't know."

Quinn's voice breaks my running thoughts. "I'm toying with the idea of meeting with the ex to get his side of the story. I'll let you know what I decide. Also, Sgt. Foley believes that the death of Laird O'Connor is the result of him running into problems with the Irish mob."

That reminds me of my uncomfortable encounter with the sergeant, "What? Why'd he ever think that?"

"Well, Sgt. Foley said he heard that his Lairdship had money problems and had borrowed heavily from the mob in Dublin to cover his shortages. Also, that the Laird had failed to pay all the money back in a timely manner, so they killed him."

I scrunch up my face and shake my head negatively, "In my experience the mob makes an example of a person whose behind in payments and tends to hurt the person versus killing them. A dead person doesn't pay money back."

"Foley feels that the mob is going to expect the Laird's son will now be more willing to pay off his father's debts."

I'm skeptical, "Why? What's the motive? The old man's good name? Laird O'Connor seems to have done damage all by himself. Do you have any contacts in the Dublin police to check the theory out?"

"That I've done. There's a friend on the Dublin police, but I'm waiting for his call back. By the way there'll be a reading of the Laird's Will on Tuesday at 10 a.m. and it could be interesting to attend."

"I'll check with Karen regarding our plans, but I hope to be there."

"This situation just gets more complicated, which leaves us both with more unanswered questions." Quinn runs his hand through his hair.

"Well, I'm gonna call it a day."

"I was wondering if you and your wife have plans for this evening?"

"I don't think so but let me check with Karen. What did you have in mind?"

"You've been a great help, I'd like to invite to my house for a light dinner and a lot of thanks."

"I'll call Karen and let you know." A few minutes later, I say, "We're free tonight. Give me your address and a time and we'll be there."

"Brilliant." Quinn replies. I head home to meet Karen and get ready.

Karen and I arrive at Quinn's apartment on the second floor above the Ballyram Angling shop. Fishing is something I've always thought I'd like to try, maybe when I have some time. Hooks, rods, and nets droop, swoop and dangle against the window. I open the door set in a slightly sagging frame at the corner of the building. A single low-watt bulb at either door resembles spot lights. The stairwell is steep and narrow with too many steps, and no place to hide if someone starts shooting. Cops never like enclosed spaces with limited escape routes. I shake it off and grab the stair rail that jiggles loose from the wall. Halfway up we encounter a thermocline of warmth and the scent of . . .

Karen turns, "I think we're having pizza."

"It smells great. My stomach was growling before; now I'm really hungry. Hopefully he has beer, too."

"You know, we haven't had pizza since we've been here. This should be fun." She knocks, and Quinn quickly opens the door, "Come in. Glad you could make it."

Karen hands Quinn the latest attempt at the Very Fruity Pie recreation for dessert this evening.

Stepping into the apartment, the warmth and smell of pizza wraps around me. I do a quick assessment. Can't shake old habits. It's one large room, furniture herded into groups to separate areas by function. Since large is not that large, one can eat, sleep, watch television, and sort laundry in a few steps.

I see a 60-inch flat screen television, a beat-up couch, a well-worn dining table with four different chairs, and a double bed, more or less made with mismatched sheets. Two sheets are flung over the poles to form curtains, and another is tacked to the far wall. "This is very nice," Karen gushes. Karen takes the intact cane-back chair. In case the rest of the furniture is fragile, I take the metal folding chair with 'St. Patrick's Reception Hall stenciled in fading navy paint on the seat back. Quinn straddles a wooden chair missing a back spindle.

"What can I get you to drink?" Quinn asks, "I have Guinness on tap."

"I'll have a Guinness."

Karen asks for a diet cola. Quinn brings us our drinks and then pulls two pizzas out of the oven, "There's cheese or cheese and sausage.

We fill our plates and begin to eat. The first bite tells me frozen pizza tastes the same in Ireland as the U.S. It's true bachelor food. I can't take my eyes off the sheet on the wall, "What's that?"

Quinn blushes a deep red, "Something I'm working on."

"Can I see?"

"Sure," Quinn removes the sheet. Names of suspects are taped to the wall. Under each name is a positive motive, means, and opportunity. His own personal, room-sized flow chart. There are a few smudges where he's added information after he taped up the papers, using the wall for stationery.

I cross the room for a closer look, "I'm duly impressed. Who do you think is the most likely suspect?"

Karen shakes her head and laughs, "I see it now. The evening has just turned into a game of 'Clue.' Who killed Laird O'Connor on a dark road with Brian Flynn's car?"

I brighten up and wave a piece of pizza at the wall. "Hey, yeah, I like that. We can do that. If the three of us talk this through, it'd give me . . . I mean Quinn, a better direction for the investigation."

Karen snorts, "Nah, you had it right the first time with the word 'me.' Okay I'll play. I'm sure it will be fun, but we civilians talk about other things than murder." Karen sighs and visibly relaxes her shoulders, "Fine. I'm gonna need a soda and another piece of pizza for this. Let's get started."

Quinn grins from ear to ear.

"Can we separate the wall into 'most likely' and 'less likely' because that would help me better visualize what we have at the end of the evening." Karen asks.

Quinn and I agree with the suggestion.

Karen takes the lead, "I would move Michael O'Connor to the 'less likely' wall. It seems unlikely his father would agree to meet him on a dark road in the middle of the night when Michael could come to the Manor on some excuse. And how would he know that Brian Flynn would be passed out drunk with keys in his car? I don't see it."

"Maybe there's insurance money for him," I interject.

Karen doesn't miss a beat, "Even then there would be a number of easier ways to kill his father that wouldn't raise suspicion."

Quinn shoots me a sideways glace. I nod affirmatively, "Yes, my wife is a dangerous woman after all the years of living with me and hearing about my cases. I'm tempted to sleep with one eye open."

We both look at Karen, who gives a coy shrug and feigns shyness, "Are you two joining the discussion?"

I jump in, "Yes. I'd move Diedre Flynn to 'less likely.' She does have means and opportunity with access the Brian's car, but what's the motive? We don't know if the rumor of her affair with Laird O'Connor is true. She seems to love Brian and I find it hard to believe she'd implicate him in the murder. Also, would she dislike the Laird enough to kill him? I don't buy it."

I can see Karen nodding in agreement. Karen adds, "Move Kathleen to the 'less likely.' She had strong feelings about Laird O'Connor moving the rocks that she believes the fairies live in, but I don't see her as the murdering type."

Quinn moves both profiles to the 'less likely' section of the wall, lifting some plaster with the tape.

We are left with Maeve Kelly, Timothy Clarke, Fionnuala Lynch, Charles O'Leary and Colleen Moore. Karen and I look at Quinn who offers, "I like Ms. Moore for it. She has a low tolerance for cheating men in her life. She tried the same thing on her husband. She spent enough time in the village to possibly know about Brian's drinking. She'd know where to find his car. I doubt she'd have any remorse in implicating Brian."

"I don't get the feeling she did it. She has too much to lose. If she waited until after the wedding, she too could've killed the Laird in a way that would raise less suspicion."

"Quinn, why do you have Timothy Clarke on the wall?" Karen asks.

"Well, you know that Tim hates Brian over the death of his son, Paddy, and he accused Laird O'Connor of raping his daughter, Moira."

"How old was she?" I ask.

"Nineteen. It was very sad, indeed. She died shortly after she moved to England to start a new job."

"Was it suicide or an accident? What caused her death?" I ask. More unravelling in this quiet village.

Karen gasps, "That breaks my heart."

"I can't remember exactly." Quinn frowns as he tries to recall the details. "I think she got sick or hurt and died on the way to the hospital. I could ask me mum. She would remember more than me."

Looking at Quinn, "I know that we didn't think Tim was capable of doing it, but could he be?"

"There's a saying in Ireland, "Beware a patient man's anger.' I know his resentment toward Brian hasn't diminished with time. If he has the same feeling toward his Lairdship, then yeah, I think it's possible."

"He definitely moves to 'most likely.'" I sit down and sip what's left of my beer. We need to gather the needed information without letting on that Quinn and I view him as a prime suspect.

"Worst thing to do is focus solely on one suspect." Turning to Karen, I ask, "Who do you like?"

“Fi. There is something I don’t like about her. She seemed very friendly with Laird O’Connor at his party. We know she was angry with Brian for going back to his wife. I think she’s capable.” Karen replies.

I spin around to face Karen, “I don’t think you can just decide she’s on the ‘most likely’ list because you don’t like her. Her alibi checked out. William Jones backed up her story that they were in bed together from the time she arrived home after Laird O’Connor’s party until the next morning.”

“But it doesn’t prove Finnoula was in bed all night. Okay, for now she can be on the ‘most likely’ wall until we know for sure that her alibi is solid. There’s always the unknown factor, the one person who no one suspects and yet has a hidden motive for committing the crime,” Quinn adds.

Karen delivers a good point, “Great sex makes for a good alibi. Even mediocre sex can make a man willing to perjure himself.”

Quinn serves up slices of pie and cups of coffee.

Karen takes her first bite and shakes her head, “Darn. It’s still not right. At least it’s not as sweet but the flavor isn’t right. I’ll try it again tomorrow.”

I jump in to answer Quinn’s questioning looks, “Karen has been challenged to discover Mary O’Neil’s ‘secret’ ingredient in her Very Fruity pie.”

Quinn nods affirmatively.

“What about the ‘Angry Farmer’?” Karen asks between sips of coffee.

Quinn’s brow furrows, “Who?”

“Sorry, that’s what Karen and I call Charles O’Leary. He

accused me of working for Laird O'Connor. He made it clear he disliked the man."

Quinn laughs, "O'Leary has been 'angry' for as long as I've known him, and I'm surprised no one has ended up dead before now."

Karen chimes in, "But his wife did say he was out of the house the night His Lairdship was killed. He'd have known about Brian's drinking and where to find his car."

"But Oona did tell you that Charles has problems driving since his stroke." I reply. "Maybe move him to 'less likely,' but Quinn you may want to still question him to try and rule him out."

Quinn nods and then adds, "For a small village we're not at a loss for suspects. I'm sorry if this ruined the evening. I really did invite you just to be social."

I'm finishing off the last sallow of my coffee when Karen stands up, "It's fine, Quinn. Dan loves this stuff and I love him. Pizza was great, and it was more fun than I expected."

"Keg's always tapped for you, Dan," Quinn answers. "And I'd be lying if I didn't say that I enjoyed meself and the ideas. We'll solve this yet."

Karen and I say good-bye and thank-you before heading out to the shooting-gallery stairs that await us for the trip back down. Karen holds my hand as we walk to the cottage.

Karen stops in her tracks as we enter the kitchen; she's staring at a vase of flowers on the counter, "Those weren't here when we left."

"Maybe they're another gift from someone," I reply.

"Didn't you lock the doors before we left?" Her eyebrows knit in a frown.

"You're right. Has anything been taken?"

Picking up the card, Karen shakes her head, "I doubt anything was taken. I think whoever it was left a warning because the card reads 'Leave it alone,' and the vase is filled with Marigolds and Yew branches. I know flowers. All flowers have a symbolic meaning, such as love, beauty and so on. Both of these can symbolize sorrow or death. You're apparently making someone nervous by helping Quinn."

"This is getting interesting. I'll check the perimeter for signs of forced entry. I'll call Quinn and have him investigate. Maybe the person left a fingerprint on the note or the vase, something. Either they have a key or it's easy to get in."

"Neither thought comforts me. I spend a lot of time alone here. I don't want to live in fear." Karen places her hands on her hips.

"You're right. I'll do whatever is necessary to make this right. I think a change of locks is in order."

Karen faces me and sighs, "I'll be in the bedroom until Quinn gets here."

I call Quinn and give him the situation. He agrees to come over now. I scan through our list of suspects and wonder which one of them would send a message using flower symbols?

Chapter 16

After a late-night waiting for Quinn to finish processing the flower vase, note, and general scene, I'm at the hardware store when it opens this morning to get a new dead bolt lock to install with keys for Karen and me only. I'll inform the reality company after I learn who did this. I have two days to assist Quinn, but when our son and his family arrive, my time will be committed to the family.

"You're sure you'll be okay here alone while I'm with Quinn?" I ask tentatively.

"I'll be fine. I think it was a warning, more than a threat. I doubt anyone would try something during the day."

"Quinn asked for a rush on any evidence found. However, after talking to him last night, it looks like whoever left the 'gift' was careful. The vase is fairly generic and has no fingerprints. He eliminated us from prints on the door and the rest were smudges. He's going to check local florists for any recent purchases of that type of flowers."

"Well, the flowers are generic too. Maybe he'll get lucky. Go and try to figure out who's behind this." Karen leans in for a kiss.

I thank Karen for being my partner in every way, even at times when she'd rather not. I make my way to the village.

First a stop at the Second Byte for a large Americano with two extra shots—maybe after last night it should be three. Entering the shop, I see Ralph sweeping up the remains of one of his front windows.

I stop dead in my tracks, "When did this happen?"

Ralph shakes his head and sighs, "It was like this when I came in this morning."

"Any idea who did this?" I say, pointing to the glass on the floor.

Ralph waves his hand in a dismissive gesture, "Nothin' to worry about. It's just a misunderstanding."

"What do you mean?"

"It's a situation that I need to do something about. I thought not doing anything would make the situation settle down and go away, but I guess I'll have to deal with it or call the Garda. Now, what can I get you?"

I order a double Americano and wait near the counter. The only other customer in the store leaves. When Ralph hands me my coffee, he lowers his voice and says, "You're a retired police detective, right?"

I look around, confused by why he's whispering, "Yes."

"I need this to stay between us. This is a small village, and I'm somewhat of an outsider to begin with. I don't need to alienate anyone else."

"Go on," my coppy sense is intrigued.

"I think this situation involves Tim Clarke. He's gotten it in his head that I was involved with his daughter Moira before she left for England and that I was the reason she left."

"Okay. Were you involved with her and/or were you the reason she left?" I inquire.

"No!" Ralph snaps, "Moira was a sweet, mixed-up teenager

when I first met her. She and her friend Nora started coming for coffee. Later it was just Moira. She came in to talk." At my raised eyebrows, Ralph continues, "Just *talk!* She was lonely. She'd gotten involved with some guy. I know he was older, and I think he may've even been married. She never said his name."

Between sips of my coffee, I ask, "So what happened?"

"For a while she was very happy then slowly things started to change, until she was just miserable. She came in one day and said that she couldn't bear to be near him and not be with him, so *she* decided to move to England. She said it would be a fresh start."

"So, you think that Tim caused this damage because he thinks you gave Moira the idea to move away?"

"I know he blames me. He told me to my face that I was the one who gave Moira the idea. I've tried to explain that I didn't, but he won't listen." Ralph drops his head.

I take a deep breath in and let it out, "Have there been other incidents?"

"I get phone calls in the middle of the night that hang up when I answer. I'd change my phone, but it's a small village and sooner or later everyone knows your business."

"My advice would be to make a report of this. You don't have any proof of who did this, but you need to have an official record of this. If it is Tim, why start up again?"

"It's comin' up on the anniversary of Moira's death. I'll call the Garda and make a report without naming names. Thanks, Dan."

I pick up my lukewarm cup of coffee and head for the Garda station. Entering the constabulary, Quinn waves me in,

"I have Charles O'Leary in an interview room. Watch from the observation room, okay?"

I nod and make my way to observation. Quinn enters the interview room, "So Mr. O'Leary, do ya know why I asked here?"

"Cuz you're an eejit. Nothin' I can help with. Am I free to go?" O'Leary starts to stand up.

Quinn sits back in his chair and folds his arms across his chest, "No, that's not the reason. You've been heard makin' threats against Laird O'Connor and now the man's dead. That's why we're here."

"You call him a man? A man doesn't lie, cheat, and steal. So, don't be callin' him a man to me and I'd never help ya' find who did this to that good fer nothin'."

"Tell me more about how his Lairdship lied, cheated, and stole?" Quinn asks calmly.

"Himself lied about where his property ends and mine begins. Cheated because he tried to buy some of me land, and all the time, he was making a deal to sell it to a developer for three times what he was gonna pay me. Stole, he stole me own son by offering him more money than the lazy, good for nothing was worth!"

"Well, those sound like powerful motives. I have it on good authority that you were gone from your house during the time we believe his Lairdship was killed. Where were you?" Quinn inquires.

"Out. No witnesses, but I don't need none. I know you and that fancy pants American detective got no evidence on me or you'd be chargin' me. I don't have to stay here and answer no more of your questions. I'm leaving cuz I have nothing to fear. You're as stupid as Foley. Neither of you could be findin' your arse with both hands. Brilliant you aren't." O'Leary stands and limps his way to the door.

"You're right, I don't have enough to charge ya, but if you hear of anything that could be help to this investigation, I'd like a call. However, don't leave the village without letting the Garda know."

O'Leary places his hand on the door knob and turns to face Quinn, "Eejit. Where exactly do ya think I'd be goin'? You're replacin' Foley as the 'lead detective' in the village. Well, heaven help us. Criminals will flockin here because they've nothing to fear from the Garda." O'Leary smiles as he turns to leave, "Whoever hit Laird O'Connor may just get away with it. Sounds like justice served to me. His Lairdship got want he deserved." He proceeds out of the station.

I wait until Quinn joins me in the observation room and say, "Well, he has enough anger, but I'm not convinced he could physically do it." Quinn nods silently. I make eye contact with Quinn and say, "I think there are a few things we need to talk about. One being the comment Fi made about you knowing if she's good in bed."

"Shhh, not here." Quinn looks around as if someone might be listening, "I'll give the name of a place we can meet later."

Quinn requests that we meet at the Sly Fox in Greengrass, a small village twenty miles from Ballyram. As I enter the pub, I spot Quinn at a back table. "Thanks for meeting me here. The pubs in Ballyram have too many ears and wagging tongues."

I nod. Quinn has a pint in front of him and has ordered one for me, so I sit down and bluntly say, "I've heard rumors and need to be sure of a few things. First, how close are you and Brian Flynn?"

"I know him and feel he's a good bloke, despite his problems with drinking, but we aren't best mates."

"Do you feel you can investigate this situation impartially?" I lean forward, making direct eye contact with Quinn.

"Exactly what have you heard?"

"That you're under pressure to solve this case, but you're too close to Brian to see the whole picture. I need to know if that's true."

"Who did you hear that from?"

"That's not important. I need you to be honest with yourself and with me about being objective and letting the evidence lead the investigation, not your personal feelings. Can you do that?"

"I can. I know Brian's history, facts and gossip, but this is about my integrity. I need to face myself every day and know I did the best job possible to seek the truth. Whoever did this must go to trial. They committed murder! This isn't about friendship."

My shoulders shift under the relief. "Okay. I'll back you and help in any way possible."

Quinn takes a long pull on his pint, "You should know that about four years ago I was involved with Fi."

"And?"

"Well, it was fairly intense, both physically and emotionally for me, at least until Ralph Santini arrived in the village. Fi dropped me because the rumor was that Ralph was a rich American, and she started chasing him about five minutes after he arrived."

"What were your thoughts and feelings about Fi at that time?"

Quinn sighs, "I was hurt, for sure. I was so easily disposed of, but the more I thought about it, the more I realized that she was never going to be the woman I'd spend the rest of my life with. Fi was a lot of fun, but she was always focusing on money, how much someone had, how to get more, and the like. In the end I was fine with the relationship ending. Then she dropped Ralph when she found out he didn't have as much money as she thought. I just wanted you to know."

"Investigations don't work unless they're based on honesty." I lean back and sip my beer. "Change of subject, what made you become a cop?"

Quinn sits back against the chair, "Me granddad was a Garda and he made it to captain before retiring. You?"

"My choice was a bit more round about. When I finished high school, I worked several jobs but nothing exceptional. I needed a job, so I joined the U.S. Army and did four years in the Infantry. When I got out I went into private security and that was good for about four years, but I needed to make a decision about a career. I felt that policing was a natural choice given my background. My grandfather hated the idea of my carrying a gun, and worse, the thought I'd use it. I felt bad that he didn't approve of my career choice. He was a great influence in my life. Before he died he told me he was proud of the man I'd become." For a moment, I smile at that memory. I turn my focus back to Quinn, "A question, why is the police force called the Garda?"

Quinn laughs, "Well, it's a bit of a history lesson that new recruits have to learn. Back in the early 1820s policing in Ireland was formed on a regional basis called the County Constabulary, then in the 1830s the Irish Constabulary was formed as well, which later still became the Royal Irish Constabulary. When Ireland became the Irish Free State in 1922, the Royal Irish Constabulary was disbanded, and the Garda Siochana was formed."

"What does that mean?"

"Garda Siochana means Guardians of Peace. It's the national police service."

I buy the next round of pints, and Quinn and I spend the next hour exchanging police stories before heading home.

Once home, I smell something sweet, Karen is in the kitchen. "Are you making another pie?"

"I'm still trying to master it. I went to Doyle's grocery, but he's not aware of what Mary uses. Tom said that he hasn't been ordering anything for her. He knows the pie I'm talking about. He says she's always closely guarded the recipe. I tried adding apricot preserves to the mix. Try a piece and tell me what you think?"

"Sure! I'm the man for the job." I take a bite and my tongue crinkles. Not in a good way.

"Well?" Karen is anxious.

"This isn't it either."

Karen sighs, "I just can't put my finger on what she adds. I'll do some more research to see if I can discover something."

I don't want to hurt Karen's feelings, but I'm not sure how many more pies I can eat. I do love pie, but there comes a time when a change in dessert is desirable. All I can hope for is that she figures out the "secret" soon. I wonder if I can get up during the night for a pie snack and quietly feed a few slices into the garbage.

Chapter 17

I'm awake at 4 a.m. because there's something I'm missing and it's so simple that once I realize it, the entire case will come together.

There's muttering from under the covers, "I can feel you thinking over here. It's like radiation and you're glowing! I know this case is on your mind, but I'd like to sleep a little longer."

"I'll try and tune my thinking down, so you can go back to sleep."

"Thank you," Karen says into the darkness of the room.

"You know that today is the reading of Lord O'Connor's will. I wonder if there are any surprises contained in it."

Karen rolls over, faces me and sighs, "*This* is tuning it down?"

"Sorry, never mind. I'll stop now," I say before doing some deep breathing and fall back to sleep but only for an hour. I decide I'm done sleeping and get up.

A couple hours later, Karen comes out of the bedroom and finds me sitting at the kitchen table reading the newspaper, "Are you attending the reading of the will with Quinn?"

"I was. We don't have any plans, do we?"

"No, but if you spend much more time with Quinn, I'm going to think one of two things. You're either been hired as a new constable or you and Quinn are secretly dating." Karen laughs, hugging me from behind.

"Wow, that's mean. I haven't spent that much time with Quinn."

"I think you must have done something wrong in a former life and are making amends in this life because you're working really hard at finding justice, but I'm suffering right along with you."

"It's Karma. I was probably a criminal or at least a really bad person in a former life and now I catch criminals. Cosmic justice."

"So, it's like a credit score, but with Karma? I should've asked your Karma score before I married you. Do you have an idea when you might improve your Karma score to the point of being able to truly retire?"

"Not a clue. It's just my lot in life, baby! Think of it like being on an amusement park ride. Sit back and enjoy!"

Karen snorts a laugh.

"I'll finish up what I'm doing and promise to be available to you for whatever you wish to do to me." I wiggle my eyebrows in a sexually suggestive manner.

Karen replies flatly, "Seriously, that's the best you can say?"

"Well, if I could get lucky, I'll do my best to extricate myself from the situation and come home. Okay?"

"It would be nice to see you, but first see Quinn and hear the reading of the will. Don't forget that tomorrow we're driving to Dublin to pick up the kids."

"I remember. No problem." Our son, Eric, his wife, Megan, and our granddaughter, Hannah, are arriving tomorrow for a two-week visit. Karen and I have been looking forward to their visit. If I miss this event, I'll be the next victim with a very short list of suspects.

I walk into the village. I stop and pace out probable events on the roadway. Visions of the scene return along with the smell that blood leaves in the air. The placement of the Laird's body means he didn't try to move to the shoulder of the road, which most people do instinctively when a car approaches. The look on his face was a mixture of shock and betrayal. Laird O'Connor knew who was coming and he expected them but didn't fear them. Who would that be? That's the question I keep coming back to. When I enter the station, Quinn is sitting at his desk.

"Top of the morning,' Sergeant Quinn"

"You do realize we don't say that in Ireland, right?" Quinn inquires, scrunching up his face.

"Sorry, an attempt at early morning humor. Are we still planning to attend the reading of the will for Laird O'Connor?"

"Yes, we'll leave in twenty minutes."

The lawyer's office building is stone, faintly cast with dirt and moss. It's one of the older buildings in the village, from the 1800s. The office is distinguished with dark paneled walls, legal textbooks mostly in modern sets, but some with leather flaking on the spines. Eight leather arm chairs are set up in two rows facing the desk. The air in the room smells as if it's from the 1800s: thick, damp, and earthy. Michael O'Connor, Colleen Moore, Fionnoula Lynch, and several of the Manor's staff are present. When I see the attorney, I think maybe he moved in when the building was new. I lean to Quinn and ask, "How old is the attorney?"

Quinn whispers, "The term is 'Solicitor' and I don't know for sure. Mr. Donnelly was a friend of me father, and he looked that old when I was growing up."

Mr. Donnelly silently lays his fingers on the desktop. They look as dry as his voice, thin and bony. His eyes catalog each person before he speaks, "I, Laird Arthur O'Connor, being of sound mind and . . ."

Michael O'Connor interrupts, "Can we just stipulate that the legal formalities are present and skip to the end?" Mummers of agreement can be heard.

Mr. Donnelly concedes, "Very well. Laird O'Connor updated his will just two months ago. He made several bequeathments: The first is the Manor estate to his son, Michael, with the caveat that he deserves it only as a birthright not through any work he has done on the land.

"Second, there is a small cash benefit to each of the staff at the Manor of 1,000 Euros each.

"Third is a cash benefit to Ms. Fionnoula Lynch in the amount of 2,000 Euros as gratitude for her friendship over the past five years. There are five or six very small contributions to local charities none of which exceeds 100 Euros."

Fi begins to cry and mutters, "I can't believe this, I can't believe this," and leaves the room. Her wispy black garments flutter as she stomps toward the door, and her black and gold jewelry jingle when she pulls it open.

Quinn and I stare at each other with that 'What do you think that means' look.

Colleen Moore stands up and says, "He left nothing to me after all the money I loaned him and the promises he made to me." She turns the Michael, "You did this! You made sure you came out on top. Someone *is* going to pay me back!"

Michael dryly smiles, "It won't be me because I don't have any money."

Colleen spits out, "We'll see about that. You'll be hearing

from my solicitor. I'll contend that he wasn't in his right mind when he signed this will." The door slams on her way out.

Michael looks at Quinn and me and sarcastically mutters, "That went well. Obviously, she loved him."

The solicitor folds his hands on the desk. "That is all. You are free to leave."

Michael's already pulling away from the curb in his BMW by the time we reach Quinn's Garda vehicle. Maybe he doesn't want the gravel of Ballyram to leave nicks. Quinn and I head back to the station to discuss what happened at the solicitor's office. Quinn appears most interested in Fi's reaction by asking, "What do you think she meant with 'I can't believe this?' She tried to make us believe that she wasn't interested in being Lady O'Connor and the rumors were wrong. She also said that she knew her relationship with the Laird wasn't exclusive, but her reaction today coupled with the statement from Colleen Moore about the row Fi had with Laird O'Connor the night of his death lead me to believe otherwise. So is there something else or was she just very convincing in her acting."

I agree, "She's a good actress, I'll give you that. Maybe she thought at some point the Laird would come to his senses and until then she would just play her options."

"I think another interview with Fi would be prudent."

"Ah, okay. I'm not available tomorrow. Karen and I are picking are kids up from the airport."

"I'll see if Fi will join us on Thursday, if that's okay?" Considering how he's being pressured by his supervisors to wrap up this case, I've just received a clear sign of how much Quinn wants me involved.

"I'll have to let you know. The kids being here adds a whole new level of balancing my availability. Call me and let me know what time she's coming in and I'll let you know if that time works." I put my hand on the doorknob when a thought returns to me, "Did you ever get additional background on Ms. Moore?"

"I spoke to my friend on the Dublin Organized Crime Task Force, who reported some interesting information. Sergeant Foley may not have been so wrong. He stated that Ms. Moore's ex-husband is reportedly second in command of the Irish mob in Dublin. His name is Shaun Daley.

Leaning forward I ask, "Who's number one?"

"Michael Daley, Shaun's older brother. Of course, the family denies being anything except honest business people. Ms. Moore went back to using her maiden name after the divorce. I also asked about the domestic disturbance incident and was told there was nothing there to be discussed."

My curiosity is piqued. "I wonder if someone a little higher up the police force decided that."

Quinn nods, "That was my thought, but I wasn't about to push it."

"May mean nothing at all, may indicate motive. We'll have to wait and see. It could show a possible pattern of behavior."

As I exit the station, I remember I promised to meet Karen at the Second Byte after her lunch date with Maeve and Kathleen. When I arrive, there's a tour bus parked out front. Inside, Karen is alone with a coffee in front of her. I wave to her, then get in line behind several Asian tourists. When I make my way to the counter, Ralph says, "Crazy busy morning. But I never turn my nose up at the tourist business. What can I get you?"

I order my usual double Americano and sit next to Karen.

Karen leans into me and whispers that she has gossip that involves Ralph, "He accused Laird O'Connor of cheating him when he bought the building."

"That must have been years ago. I wonder how he feels after all this time. Are you ready to head home now?"

Karen shakes her head, "I need to go grocery shopping. First, I'd like to find some vitamins for myself, so I'll be in the health food store here for a few minutes. Do you need anything?"

"No, I'm fine. I need to have a chat with Ralph. I'll meet you at Doyle's."

Ralph looks surprised to see me at the counter again so soon, "Back already??"

"Ralph, do you have a few minutes to sit down and talk?"

Ralph sloshes coffee into the first mug he grabs and joins me at a table at the back of the store. After Ralph sits down, I say, "I need to ask about your relationship with Fi."

"Yeah, I figured you'd be around." Ralph stares at the table. "Well, it was intense. A complete ego flatter and I fell for it. I was new in town and learned quickly that strangers are not easily welcomed, when suddenly this young, beautiful girl was all over me. She acted as if I was the most interesting person in the world. I was eatin' it up and very happy."

"And?"

"Over time I learned that she wasn't the person I thought she was. More and more of her conversations were about the money. How much I had, would have, could have, you get the idea. I heard the rumor that she was seeing me because she was on the rebound from someone else, who's married."

"So, what happened?"

"Well, she dropped me when she realized I put all my money into this place. I heard rumors that she was trying to start somethin' with Brian Flynn. I realized marital vows don't mean anything to Fi. I was pretty angry. I thought we had something special."

"Did you blame Brian Flynn for ruining the relationship?"

"I guess at first, but with time I realized Fi sees men as a tool to be used and abused for her financial gain. She was hunting for a rich husband. I wasn't it."

"Also, what is the relationship between you and Laird O'Connor?"

"He owned this building when I first came to town. My cousins rented because they never had the capital to buy the building for themselves. When I arrived in town I had enough money to buy the building. That's apparently why Fi thought I had money."

The biggest motivators for murder are love, hatred, and money. Ralph was right in the middle of both. "Did you feel that Lord O'Connor was dealing fairly with you when you bought this building??"

"I heard cops never ask questions that they don't know the answer to." Ralph stares into his coffee, drumming his fingers on the side of the mug, "I'm sure you heard that I complained that Laird O'Connor cheated me. I admit it. I think he bribed the assessor to say the property was worth more than it was. I couldn't prove that, it was just a feeling."

"What are your feelings now?"

"I've let all that go. It's behind me. I have enough income to be happy. I hope you're not looking at me as a murder suspect. If I had wanted either the Laird or Fi dead, I would've done it years ago. Same with Brian. I'm aware of his drinkin' and driving after pub closing, but my issues with him were resolved years ago as Fi moved on to other men."

I thank Ralph for his honesty. I understand that both situations are years old, but 'Revenge is a dish best served cold.' So, was it over? Or had the opportunity just recently presented itself for Ralph? Time will tell. I finish my coffee and get another to go. As I leave, I shake Ralph's hand and head over to speak to Quinn.

Quinn listens to my information about Ralph, "It seems far-fetched to wait years. Brian's drinking and driving bein' common knowledge and what would Ralph have to say to Laird O'Connor that would entice him out so early in the morning?"

I agree, "Ralph as a suspect is doubtful, but just in case, keep him on the radar."

It suddenly dawns on me that I completely forgot about meeting Karen at Doyle's Grocery. I excuse myself and hurry over. Karen is sitting on a bench in front of the store with four bags of groceries and that 'I've been there, done that' look on her face. I begin my apology fifteen feet away as I walk toward here.

Karen rolls her eyes, "You've never learned to tell time, that's your problem. Let's go home. I'm starving. You talk to Ralph?"

"Yeah, Quinn and I seem to be adding suspects instead of eliminating them."

"For dinner, I have steaks, potatoes and my latest version of the pie."

Internally I cringe, but I verbalize, "Sounds great."

Chapter 18

The morning drive to Dublin intrigues me. Mist makes the green even more striking and the brown more mysterious. I slow at the corners, not willing to nick the car against a stone wall. The drive from Ballyram to Dublin is three or so hours long and the flight with our family arrives at 8 a.m. The countryside rolls by as does the time. I get lost in thought. This case feels as if the answer is just in reach. Suddenly Karen asks, "Where are you going?"

"I don't know." I say, realizing we've arrived in Dublin.

"Well, the exit we need for the airport is right here!"

I make an assertive lane change in order to be in the right lane. Karen is severely pressing the imaginary brake on the floor of her side of the car. I calmly report, "Trust me. I'm a professional driver. I've spent years driving fast and making furtive lane changes without incident."

Karen slowly turns her head to me, "Which is fine in a police squad with red lights and siren. This is family time. Okay?"

"Hey look, we're here, on time, and in one piece. I'm a professional!"

Karen laughs out loud and stares at me.

Hesitantly I say, "What're you thinking?"

Karen leans into me and places her hand on my chest, "Right now I appear calm, while I ponder all the ways I can kill you and get away with it."

"In the meantime, how 'bout I buy coffee and a scone for each of us?"

"Fine, but I'm keeping my options open with the whole killing-you thing." A sly grin crosses her face.

Coffee and scones from an airport kiosk in hand, Karen insists that we walk to the gate, "I don't want to miss the kids when they arrive."

"They can't leave without us because I have the car keys."

We wait for about fifteen minutes and then we see them. Smiles. Laughter. Eric still looks like a college athlete, taller and leaner than I had ever been. He has Karen's coloring. Megan is blond haired, blue eyed, and lean muscle. Hannah is four years old with bouncy curls and raw energy. Karen and I wave madly when they exit customs. Eric sees us and gives us a head nod to let us know he sees us. Hannah squeals with delight, "Poppa, Nanna." She waves with so much force that she nearly strikes Eric in the head. He places her on the ground and she runs to us.

Eric says, "Hi Mom, Pops."

"How was the flight?" I ask.

"Uneventful."

Megan chimes in, "Yeah, he slept nine tenths of the way. I wasn't so lucky. Hannah fell asleep on my lap so I lost feeling in both my legs."

Once we've loaded the luggage into the car and start back to Ballyram, Karen asks, "Anyone hungry?"

We decide to have lunch at O'Neil's. Megan and Hannah fall asleep in the car on the drive.

Eric asks, "Are you liking life in your Irish village? Is it everything you thought it would be, a peaceful retreat?"

Karen laughs, "Ask your father what he has been up to."

"Okay, Pops, what are you up to these days?"

I sheepishly admit, "I sort of fell into a murder investigation."

Eric snorts and laughs, "I believe it. You'd be able to move thousands of miles away and end up being a cop. Priceless."

"I didn't mean to. Quinn is a great young sergeant that I've the pleasure of working with. He enjoys my insight."

Karen and Eric just laugh. Eric asks, "Tell me about your Irish murder."

Karen interrupts, "Please, don't encourage him. He's supposed to be retired."

Eric turns around to look conspiratorially at Karen with a wide grin on his face and replies, "Yeah, I see how well that's working out for you."

I give him a brief account of the situation to date.

"So, you have suspects. Have you been able to eliminate anyone as a suspect?" Eric inquires.

"Father Kennedy!" I reply triumphantly.

Karen's voice can be heard from the backseat, "What? You had Father Kennedy on the list?"

"Well . . . not really. Quinn learned from a reliable source that Father Kennedy was absent from the rectory during the time of the murder. So, he spoke to Father Kennedy who was able to provide a solid alibi."

Karen asks, "Who was Quinn's source?"

"Quinn's mother. She's the live-in housekeeper at the rectory since her husband passed away. She heard Father Kennedy come home from the Laird's party but didn't hear him leave during the night and thought it was strange."

Eric is puzzled, "Why is that strange? A small-town priest must get called out at night for all sorts of things."

"Right, but Mrs. Quinn said she's normally a very light sleeper and never heard Fr. Kennedy get up at all that night."

"Then why did Father Kennedy go out?" Karen asks.

"He went out to administer the 'Last Rites' to a farmer living a few miles outside the village. Quinn confirmed Father Kennedy was at the farm from about 1 a.m. until after 5 a.m. when the farmer passed away."

Karen shakes her head, "I can't believe you suspected Father Kennedy."

"Priests are people too, with all the same flaws. Quinn was duty bound to follow up when he received the information."

Two hours into the ride back to Ballyram, Megan and Hannah wake up. Hannah calls out, "Sheep, Poppa, sheep!"

"Yes, Hannah. I see them." The rolling hills and pastures pass by as we discuss possible excursions for us to take while we're together. Slowly the country road and growling stomachs lead us into Ballyram. We stop at O'Neil's.

Sean O'Neil shows us to a table and hands everyone a menu, "Who might these lovely people be?"

I introduce him to my family.

He inquires to Hannah, "How old might you be?"

Hannah holds up four fingers and proudly announces, "I'm four and a half."

Sean feigns shock, "Four and a HALF. That's old!"

Hannah enthusiastically nods her head, her hair bouncing against her t shirt.

"Brilliant. I'll give you a few minutes with the menu."

We unroll our napkins and again are amused with the sayings in each one.

Karen's says, "Live your life so your friends would readily defend you . . . but never need to."

Eric reads his, "Gratitude, like faith, is a muscle. The more you use it the stronger it grows."

Megan has, "If you live an honorable life, when you think back you'll enjoy it a second time."

Hannah says, "Poppa read mine."

"Your saying is, 'Yesterday's the past, tomorrow's the future, today is a gift. That's why it's called the present."

Hannah cocks head to one side and says, "I don't get it. Am I getting a present today?"

Everyone laughs. Eric explains that it's just a funny saying. Mine is "Experience is something you don't get until just after you need it." I think of all my cop experience and wonder how it can help this case.

One by one we decide on lunch. Karen and Megan decide to enjoy items that are an Irish specialty. My son and I think more comfort food: cheeseburgers. A hamburger for Hannah. The kids talk about some of the places they'd like to see while here. When the food arrives, we tuck in and conversations slow. I'm on my last bite when Sean appears to remove plates and inquire if anyone would like dessert.

Eric orders first, "My wife and I would like to share an order of Irish bread pudding with the warm whiskey butter sauce."

Karen says, "I'll have a piece of Very Fruity Pie."

I inadvertently shudder at the thought of pie and say, "I'll have a slice of chocolate cake."

Sean disappears back into the kitchen. Karen leans into me and whispers, "I'm so close to figuring out how Mary makes her pie. This taste should help narrow down the 'mystery' ingredient. Won't she be surprised when I tell her?"

Mary may be surprised; I'll just be relieved to have earned a hiatus from pie, but I'm not going to tell Karen that.

After lunch we drive to the cottage. "Not bad, Dad," Eric comments.

"Not bad? It's gorgeous. Just like what I thought an Irish cottage would be," Megan answers.

Hannah squeals with delight, "It's just like my book. The one with a cottage in magical woods where fairies live. Poppa, have you seen any fairies?" Before waiting for an answer, she runs inside to look around for fairies, leprechauns, and sheep.

The kids head for their room to begin unpacking. Hannah has a small cot in there as well. The din of muffled voices can be heard through the closed bedroom door. My eye catches Karen smiling as she says, "I'm glad they're here and they made it safely!"

We gather in the living room and talk about sightseeing trips again. Top of the list are Kilkenny Castle, Kiss the Blarney Stone, and visit the Cliffs of Mohr. Hannah wants to see a leprechaun and maybe even touch the pot o' gold.

I agree, "Those sound great. We'll firm up the schedule in a day or two. That'll give you some time to get over the jet lag and see some of the village."

Karen talks about the party in two days.

Eric says, "It should be fun to meet some of your new friends from the village. Leave it to mom to plan a party. I'm shocked."

"Ha ha. Luckily, you're my favorite child," Karen retorts.

Eric snorts, “I’m an ONLY child.”

“That doesn’t hurt, either.” Karen suggests a short evening walk to help us settle into the first evening together. The sun is turning the green fields into a hazy golden red. Birds chirp. Dry leave crunch under our shoes to make sounds on the roadway. The air is moist and smells of cut grass. Quiet, Irish style.

The kids are ready to recuperate from the time zone change, so by 8:30 p.m., Karen and I are left alone.

“Time for bed,” Karen yawns. “More ‘aventures’ tomorrow.”

As Karen turns toward the bedroom, I express my concern, “I know you’ve planned this Welcome party, but we could end up with a murderer in our home.”

Karen’s head drops, and she sighs, “Yes, that could be, but I refuse to live in fear. There are some really nice people here too. What would you like me to do?”

“Nothing, I’m talking out loud.”

“I can’t very well say to people, ‘You know how we had invited you to meet our family, but now that you’re considered one of the top five or six murder suspects, I’m gonna have to uninvite you. Enjoy the rest of your day.’”

“What if the murderer makes an attempt while here?”

Karen throws her hands up, “Seriously?? Do you think they’ll stab or shoot one of us and hope no one else in the room notices?”

Now I sigh, “No, of course not, but they could possibly poison one of us. Someone made a point of leaving those flowers and a note.”

“Well, it would be hard to control who gets the poison. Also, it seems that Laird O’Connor was the intended victim. Right now, neither you nor Quinn can name a suspect, so I don’t think anyone will try anything at the party."

It's my turn to throw up my hands, "You're right. In all my years of policing, I've never invited over possible murder suspects. This is just weird for me."

"I'm not dwelling on the negative things. Our family is here, and I want it to be a happy memory for all of us."

"Well, I'll be nervous and hyper vigilant the whole evening."

Karen hugs me from behind, "Fine, I can live with that. Now are you coming to bed?"

"Sure. Glad we could talk."

Chapter 19

Bacon sputters in the pan, and coffee sends its lovely smell through the kitchen. The bedroom door opens, and Hannah emerges. She's wearing a multi-colored pastel flannel nightgown. Her hair is tousled. She puts her finger to her lip to shhhs us and says, "Nanna, Poppa, we need be quiet, so Mommy and Daddy can sleep more. But today I am a princess. Want to see my princess dress?"

I wink at Karen who smiles at Hannah. Karen and I whisper, "Sorry, we'll try to quiet." I ask Hannah to help me to set the table. When the table is set, I see Eric step out of the bedroom wearing warm-up pants and a tee shirt. He's carrying fresh clothes with him, "Good morning, Mom, Pops."

"Good morning to you," Karen and I reply in unison.

Megan showers and joins us at the table. By 9 a.m. we are ready for our trip to Charles Fort. As we drive, our conversation covers Hannah's school, Irish food, and gossip from home. I find myself enjoying the break from the investigation.

At the fort, we meet our guide, Kate. She walks through the complex and says, "Charles Fort or Dun Chathail, in Irish is one of Ireland's largest forts. It's in a star shape design by William Robinson. It was built between 1677 and 1682 by the British during the reign of Charles II to protect the harbor against any foreign invaders coming in by water. However, it was vulnerable to land attacks and was taken during the siege of 1690 by William the Orange. The fort remained in services until 1922 when the British left and handed it over to the Irish government. There was significant damage in 1923 when the IRA . . ." My mind drifts. Looking into the various rooms I try to image life here on a daily basis. It must have been a struggle all the time. No central heating, thick and cold walls, food without refrigeration, and limited sanitation. I realize I'm very lucky. I need to stop obsessing about the case and enjoy this time with my family.

"Dad," Eric's voice breaks my thoughts.

"What?" I ask, and then notice the look of concern on his face.

"Where's mom? One minute she was with the group, but when the tour was over I couldn't find her."

"I don't know. She couldn't have gone far." Looking up I see Karen along the top of the forts walls. She seems to be carrying on a conversation with someone out of sight.

I nudge Eric and point, "Your mom's up there. It looks like she's talking to someone."

"She's talkin' to that lady," Hannah announces.

Eric and I both frown. Eric bends down and faces Hannah, "What lady, sweetheart?"

Bewildered Hannah answers, "The one that was crying."

"Some lady was crying?" Eric presses.

"Yeah, Nanna and I went to find the bathroom. When we were done, there was a lady in a white dress and she was crying."

"What did Nanna do then?" I ask.

"Nanna brought me back here and then went to find the lady. Nanna said she wanted to make sure the lady was okay."

I let Eric know that I'll go find Karen. When I catch up with her, I can't see anyone else, "Who were talking to?"

Karen's eyes are filled with tears, "It was the saddest story. This young girl is a military widow. She actually was only married a day before her husband was killed. She sounds so depressed that I'm really worried about her."

"What did she say?" I ask.

"Well, it was fairly mixed up. I'm afraid she was suicidal or may have some mental health disorder. I'd like to look around to see if we can find her again to see if she has anyone with her."

Karen and I do a search around the grounds but can't find the young woman she was talking to. We meet the rest of our family who say they didn't see anyone matching the description. Hannah also said she didn't see the sad lady again. We decide to leave the fort and have lunch at a local restaurant. After ordering, something is bothering me, "Karen, when you met the young woman, exactly what happened?"

Karen sighs, "Hannah and I went to use the restroom. When we came out, I must've turned the wrong way because I didn't see anything familiar. At the end of the corridor was this young woman sitting on a stair and crying. Hannah asked me why the lady was sad. We approached her to see if she needed help or if she wanted us to call someone for her. She said no and that her people are from Kinsale. She was sobbing and said she'd only been married for a day and that her husband, who was in the military, had been killed. She looked away, then right at me and said, 'Keep the ones you love close. There is danger near, especially when least expected.' She said that she was here because this is where he was stationed."

Eric breaks in, "That doesn't make sense because the guide

said this hasn't been a working fort since 1922 or something."

Holding her hands up, Karen continues, "I heard the guide say that too, but I didn't want to upset the woman any more by challenging what she was saying."

"Did she say anything else?" I prompt.

"Yes. She said that 'King John is not to be trusted as his is a false face' and then she went on to say, 'He thinks she brings him joy, but only intoxicates and turns him against his beliefs.' I didn't know what to do or say. When she saw Hannah, she stopped crying and gave her a hug and smiled. I got a little nervous because I wasn't sure if she could be dangerous, so I excused us to bring Hannah back to Eric or Megan. When I went back, she was gone. I hoped that she had just gone home or someone found her and helped her."

Hannah scrunches up her face, "I didn't like her, Nanna. That lady's hands were very cold."

I look at the brochure I picked up about the fort, "It says that this fort was built during the reign of King Charles and then taken over by William the Orange. It doesn't say anything about King John."

Megan looks up from her phone, "I just looked it up and King John ruled in the 1200s."

"So, this fort wasn't even built while King John was alive," Eric comments.

Karen nods, "Hence the reason I think she may've had a mental health issue. She seemed confused and jumbled things together. I just hope she's okay."

I hug Karen, "I'm sure people in the area know her and make sure she's okay.

Megan looks from each of our faces, "I don't know if this means anything, but I did another internet search and there a story about 'The White Lady of Kinsale.' It says that she committed suicide at the fort after her husband was killed there on their wedding night. She's said the haunt the fort to this day."

Eric shakes his head, "The woman today must have read the story and was acting it out. I find it hard to believe it was a ghostly encounter."

Megan shrugs. Lunch arrives and it's time to switch topics. We talk about the upcoming party and things that still need to be done for it.

On the drive home, Eric and I begin discussing the case. He asks if I have any clear idea who is the leading suspect.

"The biggest problem is lack of evidence. The only thing I know for sure is that Brian's car was at the scene of the crime, but there's no proof that Brian was behind the wheel. No other fingerprints in the car, either. I'm frustrated with lack of progress. I mean, I feel bad that Quinn hasn't been able to close the case."

Everyone in the car laughs.

"Priceless, Pops. But remember what I used to tell you, when you would share puzzles with me when I was in high school. Your mind knows the answer. All you need to do is look at the pieces and put them together the right way."

I fall silent and focus on my driving, but truth be known, my mind is still going over the evidence. Everyone else in the car chats away happily on future sight-seeing plans.

The day slowly turns to evening as we drive. Once home Megan takes Hannah into the bathroom for a bath before dinner. Karen looks in the refrigerator for ideas for dinner. We have a chicken, potatoes and the fixings for a green salad, and another pie. Karen says she needs to run into the village because there's no milk for breakfast.

"I'll go if you want," I offer.

"No, that's okay I want to look around Doyle's in case I see something else we need. I'll take the car and be back in a jiffy. Start dinner, please."

Dinner in the oven, Eric and I settle in to watch a movie. When Karen is back she seems distracted.

"Everything alright?" I ask as Eric and I set the table.

Cocking her head to one side, "I'm not sure. I was in Doyle's going up and down the aisles when I saw Maeve coming. I wanted to ask if there was anything new from the Beatification Committee meeting from today, so I followed her until she went in the back room. I waited by the door. She was talking to Tom, and I'm sure he handed her an envelope with cash in it. I saw her thumb through the bills.

I drop the forks on the table, "A lot of cash or a few bucks?"

"A lot and I mean *a lot*! Like 100s of dollars or would it be euros?" Karen frowns, "Why would he be giving her that much cash?"

"I don't know. I mean if he owes her money, why not write her a check, unless he believes in cash only." I scratch my chin, "The store handles cash, but that should be accounted for. Did they see you standing there?"

"No. When I saw Maeve turn toward the door, I stepped back a few feet and looked at ice cream. I tried to look surprised to see her there and then asked my questions about the committee. She seemed caught off guard with me at first and then was cool as a cucumber talking to me. She said she'd let me know if there is anything I can help with."

"Okay, as long as they didn't see you watching them. Did you see Tom?"

"Yeah, shortly after Maeve left, I was finishing up when I turned around and Tom was standing right behind me. I jumped a little and tried to laugh it off by calling him 'Ninja grocer.'"

"He say anything?" I ask.

"He stated that he saw me talking to Maeve. I waved it off as nothing important and told him the same thing about letting me know if there was anything I could help with because I had missed the meeting. I think I threw him off because I asked if he's been losing weight."

Eric snorts, "It's frightening how calm you can be in those situations. You're not a former CIA operative, are you?"

"You'll never know!" Karen laughs, "Anyway, he went on say 'yes.' I nudged him a little and commented if he was trying to impress anyone special. He melted and said that Maeve helped him see the happiness in his life. I quoted Huey Lewis and the News, 'I want a new drug. One that makes me feel the way I feel when I'm with you.' I think the pop culture reference was lost on him, so I excused myself and went up front to check out."

"If they're a couple, maybe he's just helping her out, but I'll talk to Quinn. Eric is right. You must be a CIA operative," I snicker. Karen wiggles her eyebrows at us and heads into the kitchen to finish getting dinner ready.

Dinner over, dishes done, we settle in to watch a movie. Soon after we all call it a night.

Chapter 20

After a late breakfast, Karen and Megan start setting up for the party tonight. They start setting out paper decorations along with Irish and U.S. flags. At that point, Eric and I escape with Hannah to pick up sandwich fixings. Tim Clarke smiles while tucking breads into paper bags, "I'll be seein' you tonight," he winks. "Everyone in town is interested in meetin' your family." Tim leans closer to me and lowers his voice, "Any progress you have on the case?"

"I know that Sergeant Quinn is still interviewing people."

I'm sure everyone in town is discussing the case and eyeing up their neighbors, wondering who is high on the suspect list.

We haven't been gone long enough because Karen is busy wiping surfaces and Megan is vacuuming. Eric and I set up the bar in the kitchen. There's a variety of bottled beers both from local brewers, including 6 packs of Fall N' Pumpkin and a half barrel of Guinness from the Lamb and Ram that were delivered yesterday, along with the tables and chairs.

Quinn is the first to arrive and presents us with a bottle of wine for the evening. He asks to speak to me alone. We head into the laundry room and close the door.

"I just got word that a group of investigators are comin' from Dublin in the next day or two," Quinn whispers.

"Garda Investigators from Dublin? Why?"

“Apparently there’s a ring of people stealing tourist identities here in Ballyram. So, Dublin is sending their Fraud Investigators. Sergeant Foley has been assigned to act as their liaison. Rumor I heard is that the Irish mob has been operating an identity theft ring in Dublin. The investigation has been going on for over a year and that some of the ID’s that were stolen were traced here to the village and to local shops.”

Furrowing my brows together, I ask, “Who are the suspects and why was Foley given the assignment and not you?”

“The local Brass, as you Americans say, are bein’ closed mouth about who is suspected. I think they wanted Foley to go out with a big case because he’s so close to retirement.”

“I thought your superiors didn’t like him or thought he messed too many cases up. Why give him this?”

Quinn shrugs, “Maybe with Dublin bein’ in charge, they figure Foley can’t mess it up, but can claim to be part of a big case.” Quinn smiles sheepishly.

I’m rolling this information in my head and making a list of possible suspects, when Karen knocks on the door and says, “You two okay in there?”

I open the door. Karen smiles at me, “Anything I should know about?”

I shake my head negatively, “No. Police stuff. Nothing to worry about.”

“Well, we have guests arriving. Dan, can I ask you to be on coat hanging duty?” Karen asks.

Karen and Megan finish putting out food. Eric has Hannah greeting the guests.

Mary and Sean O’Neil arrive next, cradling a covered plate,

"This is so exciting to have an evening out. I brought a Guinness Cake with whipped cream. I hope you and your family enjoy it."

Sean O'Neil presents me with a set of pictures from Laird O'Connor's party, "Dan, here's a small memento of your time in the village. I wish it were a happier memory."

I'm touched, "Thank you. That's very thoughtful of you. I'm glad you were able to make it to our party. Let me introduce you and Mary to my son and his family."

I feel awkward as more people arrive. There may be a murderer in my house or are they suspiciously absent.

By eight o'clock most of the guests have arrived. Fionnuala isn't here. Brian and Deidre Flynn had sent regrets days ago, stating that they could not leave the pub on a Friday evening. John Shea, our realtor had sent regrets saying he had a meeting in Dublin he couldn't miss. Karen and I invite people to help themselves to the buffet. Eric helps me act as bartender, so I can be make my way around the room and spend time with each guest. Hannah charms the guests with her stories of fairies she's read about and her smiles. Kathleen takes great interest in talking with Hannah and invites her to visit the gift shop, where Kathleen has a variety of fairy statues. Hannah lights up and I assure her we will visit the store. Fr. Kennedy, Quinn, and Tim Clarke are explaining the rules of Hurling to Eric, who played Lacrosse and baseball in college. They're all laughing about moments from various games and try to compare the rules of each sport. I hear Quinn explain that there is a Hurling team in Ballyram, and he invites Eric to a practice before Eric leaves the village.

Claire is explaining the latest fashion trends to Megan, as Harvey stands by his wife, smiling. Claire doesn't seem to run out of things to brag about regarding the newest collection she has arriving. Looking over her shoulder, she leans into Megan, "That is if I can keep a certain witch out of my store." Claire cackles with laughter then pats Megan's arm, "Just kidding, I love all my customers." Megan looks a bit lost for words. I wonder who the 'witch' is?

"Claire, can I get you another drink?" I ask, breaking the awkward silence.

"Yes, please. Anything red, that's all I drink." Again, I wonder if Claire's serious or being dramatic for attention? Karen is talking with Maeve and Tom Doyle about committee business. Kathleen and I join them.

Maeve asks Karen, "Have you been able to see any of the sights of Ireland?

"Not as many as we would've liked to. We've been to Fort Charles and the Blarney Castle. I really want to see the Cliffs of Mohr. I know Dan would love to visit the Guinness and Jamison factories."

Maeve shakes her head, "You need to be stayin' away from them tourist traps. That's not the real Ireland. You need to be seein' where we've lived and died to understand Ireland."

Karen graciously smiles, "Well, we're just getting started. I'm sure we'll see much more before we leave. Maybe you can give me some ideas of places."

"I'll do that for you, Karen. Brilliant."

Karen nods, "However, I really did enjoy Blarney Castle. I met a man while I was on the grounds. He told me about where blarney comes from, and then he gave me a riddle, 'The woman with white shoulders holds the key.' I've no idea what it means."

Kathleen chimes in, "Fionnuala."

Karen cocks her head to one side, "What about her?"

"No, the name Fionnuala means 'woman with white shoulders.'"

I'm speechless. Does Fionnuala Lynch truly hold the key? Did she kill Laird O'Connor or know who did?

Karen stammers for a reply, "That's, that's interesting. Thank you for the information."

Kathleen goes on, "The name comes from the Irish *fionn* which means white or fair and *guala* which means shoulder. It comes from the Irish legend that she was one of the four children of Lir, the Irish god of the sea. The children were all transformed into swans for 900 years. I study names and their meaning. I think it can say a lot about a person. Maeve means 'Joy,' Karen means 'pure.' and Daniel from the Bible means 'God is my judge."

"That's great information," Karen says.

Kathleen is not deterred. Her eyes flash with anger, "Laird O'Connor's first name was Arthur, which is a British name, meaning 'Strong as a bear.' I think he was a bear, not to consider others' feelings. He would've torn my fairies' home apart without a care."

Maeve snaps, "Kathleen, that's enough with your goin' on about nonsense." Kathleen drops her eyes and wipes tears with her napkin.

I jump in to change the subject, "Please, everyone, be sure to help yourselves to more food. We have plenty and it's delicious." Slowly conversations start up and the evening wears on. I'm preoccupied with trying to dismiss the ideas that a 'ghost' gave Karen a valid clue in this case. I wouldn't consider it if it came from anyone other than my wife. That it involves Fi's name of all the possible names in Ireland makes me even more curious. Several times I hear Karen's prompts to focus me back on a current conversation. Slowly I'm aware of people excusing themselves from the party.

By 11 p.m. Karen and the kids exchange impressions of the village while I work quietly, pondering who said what and who meant what. I tune into Karen and Eric's exchange, but keep my thoughts to myself.

"They seem like nice people," Eric comments, pulling the bag from the garbage can and tying the top shut.

"Yes, don't they," Karen replies.

But one of them is likely a murderer, I think as I take the garbage bag to back door.

Megan's washing dishes and interjects, "I don't think I'd be able to live in the same town, with the same people, my whole life. Can you imagine going through school and life seeing the same people every day?"

Karen dries each item as Megan hand them to her, "But look how cheerful they are, how kind, and how genuinely nice they are to each other."

Until they kill one another.

"True. Maybe small towns make people nicer than big cities," Eric admits.

Or not.

"Sure, like Sean and Mary. She's an excellent cook," Megan states. "I loved her Guinness cake."

"She's the one with the mystery pie, right?" Eric asks.

"Oh, your father's been telling you about my pie experiments?"

"I think he was glad for cake tonight."

Karen snorts, "I think you're right. I've been over doing pies, but I'm sure I'll figure out the recipe."

I groan silently. *I used to love pie.*

"I'd love to hear more from Kathleen. I thought her knowledge of names; their meanings and Irish legends was fascinating. I feel bad that Maeve always snaps at her. I can't believe her name means 'Joy.' I think it means 'bossy one,'" Karen says sarcastically.

"Mom be nice. You know that families have their own histories. We really don't know these people to judge." Eric cuts in, "I'm really interested in seeing a Hurling game. I have to thank Quinn for the invitation."

Karen pinches Eric's chin, "You are the thoughtful one. You're right."

Megan wipes her hand dry on the towel she's holding, "My mouth is sore from smiling."

"But they are delightful people, aren't they?" Karen asks. Everyone nods.

"And Hannah loved it all," I add.

Megan laughs, "Hannah wanted to stay up for all of the party but fell asleep two hours into it. She really wants to see fairies in the woods and find where they play. I love her imagination."

"I'd love to have Kathleen over for dinner by herself and ask her more about Irish legends. I love that kind of stuff: the myths, ghosts and fairies. I think I'll plan something before we leave. However, right now my feet hurt, and I think it's time for me to go to bed. Thank you all for a wonderful evening and all the help," Karen says as she takes off her shoes and heads for the bedroom. I'm two steps behind her.

Chapter 21

The beginning of daylight and Karen is up to put the room right. Dining room table and chairs once again a set. Clean dishes returned to their proper shelves. Decorations taken down and carefully placed in a box. I make coffee and look in the fridge for leftovers. The great thing about a party are the wonderful leftovers. I pull out a piece of Mary O'Neil's dessert and sit at the table. The over-filled fork is at my tongue when Hannah says, "Poppa, did you have breakfast? Momma says you can't have dessert until you're done with breakfast."

Busted by a four-year-old. "Well, that's a good idea. What should we have?"

"I like scumbled eggs and sasage."

"Me too. We can have breakfast together. Okay?"

"Okay."

I set about my breakfast making task. Sitting down to eat, Hannah looks at the envelope of pictures from Sean O'Neil and inquires, "What's that?" I pull the pictures out and describe the party at the manor house. Hannah's eyes grow enormous and she squeaks out, "Like a real live castle with a princess?"

"No princess, but the man who lived there was a Laird."

"Is that just like a prince?"

"Well, sort of."

Hannah points to Sean & Mary O'Neill, "Those people come

to our party. So, did he." She touches Quinn's picture and his image is now covered with scrambled egg.

"Yes, you're right."

"Who's that lady? Is she the princess of the castle?"

Fionnuala Lynch. "No, she isn't the princess, but I'm sure she would've liked to be," I mutter more to myself than anyone.

"She's pretty. I like the clips in her hair, can I get some?"

"Maybe we can go shopping and see what we can find. Ask Nanna if she wants to walk into town later?" Hannah jumps down from her chair and runs into the living room saying, "Nanna, do you want to go shopping with Poppa and me?"

I eat the last bite from my plate and begin putting the pictures back in the envelope when I hear what Hannah had said, "Clips in her hair . . . Clips?" I look at the picture and then I put on my reading glasses and take a closer look. Could the barrettes that Fionnuala is wearing be the same as the mangled clip at the scene of Laird O'Connor's death? The one Quinn and I thought was a car part, maybe a hose clip, or just another part of the accident refuse? I pick up my phone and a few rings later, I say, "Quinn, sorry to wake you this early. Dan Novice here. I think I found something interesting. Would you be able to meet me at the station in approximately an hour?"

"Ummmmm, sure. What time is it?"

"It must be about 7:30 a.m. Sorry."

He yawns into the phone, "Yeah, I can be there. What did you find?"

"I have a picture that I need enlarged. Do you have the equipment that can do that?"

"Yeah."

"Brilliant. I'll see you at the station."

I hang up the phone, still holding the picture when Karen walks into the room, "Who are you calling so early in the morning?"

"Um, ah, Qqquinnn."

She looks directly at me, her eyes narrow, and she inquires, "Why? I thought this was family time."

"I think I found an important key to the death of Laird O'Connor or at least an interesting clue. Quinn and I should investigate it further."

"Dan, I love you and I've tried to be supportive, but even I have a limit. This is getting old."

"I know, but I think this may be the break the case needs."

Silence. Karen seems pre-occupied with the kitchen floor. After what seems like an eternity, she says, "Fine, how long do you think you'll be gone?"

"One hour. Two hours, tops." I hold up one finger, but that changes to my wagging two fingers.

At the police station, I stare with Quinn at the pictures Sean provided to me from the Laird's party. "What do you think that looks like?" I quiz Quinn.

"I'm not sure—what you are pointing at?"

"Enlarge the portion of the photo with Fi's head."

Twenty minutes later Quinn and I are looking at the enlargements. He grabs the evidence bag with the mysterious clip in it. He holds the bag next to the enlarged photo of the antique barrettes that Fionnuala Lynch wore in her hair to Laird O'Connor's party. Shiny. Silver. Curved with a recurve. The 'clip' in the evidence bag matches part of the barrette in shape and pattern. Quinn whistles and laughs, "She was there at the accident scene when Laird O'Connor died! There is no other way that barrette would be there. I think we need to ask Fi to come to the station today and give us her version of how her barrette came to be found at the crime scene." Quinn picks up the phone and calls Fi's home number but gets no answer. He also tries her cell phone. Same thing, no answer. Smiling he asks, "Do you fancy a drive?"

"Yeah. It could have a simple explanation, but I think a stop at Fi's home is a good idea."

It's less than ten minutes to her home, in the opposite direction of my cottage. Fi's car is on the driveway, so she should be home. Quinn knocks, but no answer. He knocks again and rings the bell, still no answer.

He pounds at the door. Something isn't right. Both our coppy senses are on high alert.

I peek through the living room window and say, "Break the door down. It's not good." Quinn and I give the door one great shoulder smash together, and it bangs open against the wall.

Fionnoula Lynch is hanging from the second-floor railing above the living room, her face slack. There's the death smell of stagnant blood, bowel muscles released, and despair. The bitter smell enters my nose but rests in the back of my throat. I've never been to a death when I haven't caught a whiff of despair.

Quinn's hands stipple along Fi's wrist, then as he checks her neck. Nothing. I watch as he moves limbs to estimate the progress of rigor mortis and body temperature. "She's cold to the touch. She's been dead for some time." Quinn looks at me, pulls out his cell, and dials a number, "Coroner."

The breeze through the doorway ripples a piece of paper on the coffee table, the ink purple, the words loopy and large. Careful not to touch it I read out loud to Quinn,

To Whom It May Concern:

I cannot go on with living. I have lost the greatest love of my life. I gave my heart and soul to him. He held my every breath from the first time my eyes looked upon that beautiful face. He did not return the scope of my love. He broke me by his words, "I have found someone else, my true soul mate." No one can understand my never-ending pain. I am in a pit of despair the depth of which is endless. I see no other way out.

To my friends and family, I hope you can find forgiveness in your heart for my actions and the grief I have caused. Do not mourn for me. My pain is never more. May God have mercy on my soul.

"'To Whom It May Concern'? What is this, a suicide note, or a frickin' resume? It sounds like one of those old business writing books. You know, the ones that went out twenty years ago," I remark.

Quinn shakes his head, "To be sure, she was melodramatic. But even so. It's not the Fi I knew. But, it looks like her handwriting. I'll have it checked out and dusted for prints."

"It's a bunch of bull," I mutter under my breath.

"What?"

"Quinn, nobody Fi's age writes like that. Heck, I bet no one over fifty years old even writes like this."

Quinn snaps on gloves and places the note inside an evidence bag, "How do you feel about helping me process the scene?"

"I can do that."

I call Karen and briefly explained what has happened and tell her I won't be home for a few hours.

Karen gasps, "That's terrible. What a shame and a waste."

"I need to stay. It's important."

"You're right. Call me when you're on your way home, and I'll have something to eat for you. I love you."

Quinn sets his blue evidence case next to the sofa and hands me a pair of plastic gloves. Tape measure. Pad of paper. Quinn sketches what we have before it changes. I take pictures. Then, we begin investigating. My first suggestion is to reconstruct the scene. A wooden chair is lying on its side, a few feet from the victim. Quinn sets the chair upright. We have the length of rope. The distance between the noose of the rope and the chair appears too long.

I look between the chair and the length of rope, "Do you know how tall Fi was?"

"I'd say 5'4" or 5'5" at most. She couldn't have been much taller than that."

"I think you're right. However, my calculation is for this situation to be a suicide Fi would have to be at least 5'8". She wouldn't be able to stand on the chair and reach the noose to put her neck in it."

"Are you sure you measured right?"

I stand next to the chair, "I know I'm right."

"You thinkin' maybe Fi had help hanging herself?"

"Someone is working hard to make us believe she did. I've never seen a suicide note that ties up everything so neatly. Who would have the most to gain by ending the investigation?"

"Brian Flynn?"

"I still can't believe that. It's just too easy. Plus, obvious."

The rope is stained, a substance like dried blood. I suggest a DNA swab of the stain to look for possible skin cells on the rope. My hope is they're from the murderer. At least I hope so.

A single wine glass found on the living room coffee table is dusted for prints and all appear to be of one donor. Quinn also dusts an open wine bottle for prints, but none are found.

"No one wipes down a bottle in their own home," Quinn comments.

"You're right."

The coroner interrupts us to remove Fi's body and comments, "It appears to be a straight forward suicide, but I won't know for sure until after the autopsy. I'll let you know in a day or two. That's our timetable now." Maybe it's part of their training, but I never could feel comfortable with their smoothness. The coroner lays the black body bag next to Fi in the living room carpet. He and his silent, gangly assistant place Fi's body into the bag. It's zipped up and then they lift her onto the steel, wheeled gurney. Without a word between them, they remove Fi from the scene.

When he and Fi are gone, we turn to each other and start the search of the house.

A whole house that could be filled with clues or hiding one clue. We touch and turn and run our fingers along shelves, inside drawers, onto closet shelves. Fi has a closet stuffed with an amazing wardrobe. Many with tags from Le Meillure. It's when we are turning the bed, seeing nothing hidden under the mattress and nothing in the bedside table except a supply of condoms a drugstore would be pleased to offer, that the floor board gives a little under my weight. I step back and smile at Quinn.

Quinn gives me the 'You gotta be kidding' look. Under the

floor is a secret compartment boxed in by joists, holding a small square, metal box. The box is steel grey that's about 12"x12". Money? Jewelry? Drugs?

Files. Several manila file folders. I open the first one. They are not just any file, but pretty amazing and detailed files. Fionnoula apparently has "files" on a number of residents of Ballyram and their secrets.

All the evidence is bagged and tagged, then we head back to the station to process it. We first look at the files and they prove most interesting. Blackmail. There's a motive for more than a few people.

The first file is on Claire Clarke. Fi ran a background check under the guise of a home mortgage. Two years ago, Claire was arrested for shoplifting jewelry from several high-end stores in Dublin and bargained a plea deal that resulted in Claire not admitting guilt. However, she is banned from the stores for life, must return all of the merchandise, and placed on two years' probation.

"Fi had clothes from Le Meillure. I wonder if the clothes were a store write-off as payment for her silence? I think an interview with Claire will be in order for tomorrow. Don't you," I ask

The second file was on Timothy Clarke. In it is a medical report from a London clinic indicating that his daughter, Moira was pregnant. No doubt by Laird O'Connor. A cancelled check from Laird O'Connor appears to support the claim. An autopsy report indicates her cause of death was suicide in a London flat.

Quinn grunts, "I heard that Moira died in an accident. I never heard that it was suicide. The story is that she went to England for a new job."

I shrug, "I guess Tim didn't want this information to be known in the village. How old was she at the time of her death?"

"She would have been about 19."

Another file is on Sergeant Foley. Apparently when Foley was a constable he was drunk while on duty. The box has official report copies of an officer called to the scene where a pedestrian was struck and injured by a Garda vehicle. According to other officers' observations of Foley shortly after the accident, he was slurring his words, appeared disorientated, and refused field sobriety tests. The final dispensation stated that the pedestrian, who was a tourist, stepped out in front of Foley while he was answering an official police call with lights and sirens. Sgt. Foley's slurred words were due to a head injury from the accident.

"How did Fi get a hold of all this information?" Quinn wonders.

"I would image there was bribery involved, but I wonder if she also snooped through people's home and private files. I'm sure that this isn't information people look at often, so if the reports went missing, people may not have noticed at first. However, when they'd realize the information was missing it's not like people would call the police, especially if they didn't want their secrets revealed to the whole village."

"We're gaining suspects instead of eliminating them. We're going to have to interview everyone who Fi has a file on."

"But for now, I need to get home before Karen sends out a search party."

"I'll see you tomorrow for interviews with all of our new suspects."

"I'll be there."

Chapter 22

Karen had leftovers warming for me when I arrived home last night. I answered a few questions from Karen about the situations, but mostly I ate quietly. It had been a long day.

Eric, Megan, and Hannah have plans to go to Blarney Castle alone today since Karen and I had already 'Kissed the Blarney Stone." Karen was fine with us not going along, at least this time.

We walk together into the village but go our separate ways. We step out into the cool, damp air. No breeze. It mimics the mood of the walk. I hear birds all around and the scraping of the gravel on the soles of my shoes as we begin. Karen is trying not to show her disappointment that I am again on my way to a police station, so she says very little. My mind drifts to the case. Pieces everywhere, pictures of the deaths flash through my mind. Separate? Together?

I'm brought back to the present by Karen saying, "I'm interested in what they have to say regarding this situation."

I laugh, "Is a part-time investigator taking form?" Karen smiles at me. We arrive at the coffee shop. Karen gives me a kiss and a hug, whispering in my ear, "Stay safe. I love you."

"I will. I promise. I love you, too."

We plan to meet later this afternoon to compare notes. I move quickly to the station and Quinn beckons me over, "I just got off the phone with the coroner. The preliminary tox screen came in.

Fi had barbiturates in her system, enough to have killed her, but the cause of death was hanging. It doesn't seem right, but the note makes it look like she was depressed by Laird O'Connor's plan to marry Colleen Moore, and in a fit of rage, killed him, then couldn't live with the guilt of what she had done and committed suicide."

"I have a problem with the note. Are we sure it's Fi's hand writing?"

"I sent it in for analysis and it came back as consistent, more or less."

"What do you mean 'more or less'?"

"The hand writing expert confirms that it's similar enough to be Fi's and not a forgery, but there appears to be slight variations from the current sample that was submitted."

"What are slight variations?"

"The expert explained it as if the writing was older, maybe written when Fi was younger, but that can't be. She wouldn't have written about losing Laird O'Connor a few years ago and everyone in Ballyram knows that Fi ends all her relationships because she moves onto someone else."

"Were there any other fingerprints on the suicide note besides Fi's?"

"One set that hasn't been identified, but that could very well be from the person selling the paper or something like that," Quinn says, grimacing. "There's official pressure to walk away from this one."

"Does the name Foley have any connection to the official pressure?"

"No, but his boss does."

“Did the rope get sent in for DNA testing?”

Quinn winks, “Yes. If asked, I’ll remember the request to close the case came after I’ve got the test results back or maybe even a little later than that. But I’ll not be conductin’ anymore interviews with the suspects that Fi had files on. Sgt. Foley ordered me to close this case and release Fi’s body for burial.”

I keep returning to the same questions. Is it one murderer for two murders, two murders with two murderers, or a murder followed by a suicide?

My coppy senses tell me that the murder of Laird O’Connor led to the murder of Finnoula, but how to prove it. We have evidence of Fi’s presence at the scene of Laird O’Connor’s death. Was she alone or with an accomplice that felt she knew too much. Fi excelled at the self-preservation game, so in crisis, she would have turned in the accomplice. That would be a real threat to the accomplice, so that person might have turned on her first.

The next step would be to match the any DNA found on the rope to someone and hope that an answer will be revealed as motive.

I hate that feeling of incompleteness and walk slowly home to wait for Karen who arrives about 3 p.m.

Karen tells me, “Coffee was very interesting today! Kathleen and Maeve were talking about Fi’s suicide. Kathleen said that Fi lost her mother when she was only 12 years old and suicide must be a genetic thing. Her mother took a handful of pills and got into the bathtub. Fi discovered her mother’s body after school.”

“So, her mother committed suicide as well. That is interesting!”

“It gets better. Apparently Fi attempted suicide once before. She had a horrible break up with a boyfriend when she was 15.

Nora O'Brien went over to ask Fi if they could study together or something. She found her in the bathtub with empty pill containers, and the remains of a glass of wine lying on the floor next to the tub. Nora called her mother, who came over and was able to get Fi to throw up. Fi was rushed to hospital and spent time on the psychiatric ward working on a number of issues including grief, self-esteem, and alcohol addiction."

"Did they say who the boyfriend was?"

"Yeah. Believe it or not, it was Patrick Clarke, the boy who was killed in the car crash."

"Really?" My curiosity is piqued.

"Yeah, Kathleen stated that Patrick was laughing with his friends that he dumped Fi because she was too clingy. Apparently Fi heard about what he said and was so embarrassed that she attempted suicide. Do you think Laird O'Connor's announcement that he was getting married caused Fi to commit murder then use suicide as a way out?"

"It just seems too easy. Do you know if she left a note the first time she attempted suicide?"

"I asked about that, but neither Kathleen nor Maeve knew for sure. They don't remember a note being mentioned, why?"

"Quinn said there was 'slight variations as though it was older' in Fi's handwriting in her suicide note. That's just bothering me."

Karen shrugs, "Maybe she wrote it this time after taking the pills and the pills affected her hand writing."

"Maybe. My coppy sense tells me there is more to that note. Maybe it's a really good forgery. To change the subject, what's for dinner?"

"Lasagna. Eric, Megan, and Hannah will be back before it

gets too dark outside. I'll put the lasagna in before they get back."

A short time later the family is assembled at the table for dinner.

Eric looks at me and asks, "Hey, Pops, what did you do today?"

I give my standard reply, "Nothing! I'm retired."

Eric, Megan and Karen sputter, nearly choking on their food.

"What? I *am* retired, you know."

All three continue laughing. Eric replies, "*We* know you're retired. We're just not sure *you* know it. You've spent a good deal of time at the police station just since we've been here."

Hannah looks at me, "Poppa, you silly."

Everyone laughs. I know I keep promising, but I do need to make time for them while they're here. We settle in for the rest of the evening. Dessert is another version of the pie challenge, and I'm not sure if Hannah is eating hers or wearing it.

Megan is finishing up Hannah's bath and Eric plans to read books to her before bed. Karen and I are on the couch reading when there's a knock at the door. Opening it, I see Quinn, "I'm sorry to disturb you this late, but I wanted you to hear this from me. The Garda executed several search warrants in the Identity fraud case today."

I wave Quinn in, "Please come in and sit down. I'm dying of curiosity. Who, what, when, where? Any details you can share?"

"The warrants were for Tom Doyle's grocery, Maeve's Bed and Breakfast and Lace shop, and John Shea's real estate office and each of their homes. Apparently, the story about John Shea was a lie. He's been part of the Irish mob since he was a teenager. The mob sent him here to keep tabs on Tom and Maeve. His physical presence made sure they didn't forget about the deal with the devil they made."

"Why did Tom and Maeve do it?"

"They were heavily in debt. Both were on the verge of bankruptcy. Tom had borrowed from Collen Moore's former brother in law. When he couldn't pay it back, the mob worked out a unique payment plan. John moved here and had access to tourist's records and then along with the Bed and Breakfast records and Doyle's grocery, they were able to steal enough personal information and pass it along to the mob. Mob loved it. However, Tom and Maeve were also making a profit. They confessed to adding a few dollars to every purchase made by day tourists. They figured most people don't look at their receipt and if the people did, they would apologize for the mistake and refund to money." Quinn runs his hand through his hair, "I had no idea. I've known these people my whole life."

Karen checks our receipts she has, "There's nothing unusual on our receipts."

Quinn shakes his head negatively, "Tom said they only did it to people on their way out of the village. They knew you were a cop and weren't goin' risk it.

Karen throws up her hands, "That must have been the money I saw Tom giving Maeve that day at his store. I wonder if the marigolds were from Maeve, but I didn't see the money until after the flowers showed up."

"When they found out you were a cop, they didn't want to take any chances."

"I had coffee with Maeve and never suspected a thing. What about Kathleen? Was she involved?" Karen inquires.

"No. Both Tom and Maeve were clear on that. They are cooperatin' with the Garda in hopes it helps with sentencing.'" Quinn replies.

Quinn thanks us for our time and leaves. Karen and I make our way to the bedroom.

Sighing, I say, "This peaceful little village is anything but that, with murder, fraud, and theft. I wonder if Fi was part of that. Did she commit suicide because she had no way out with both the fraud and murder or did her partners help her suicide along?

"King John is not to be trusted as his is a false face," Karen mutters.

"Sorry, I didn't hear you."

"'King John is not to be trusted as his is a false face,' that's what the young lady said when we were at Fort Charles. It didn't make sense at the time. I just assumed she was mentally confused," Karen answers.

"I guess I still don't know what we're talking about."

"King John. John Shea dressed like Elvis. You know 'The King.' Hence, King John. The whole story about why he moved here was a cover story . . . a false face. She was trying to warn us not to take him at face value. I'm slow to catch on too."

Lying in bed I hear Karen's breathing slow to a deep, rhythmic pace. My mind still spins with the events of the last few days. What about Karen's encounter with the woman at the fort? How would she know about John Shea having 'a false face'? Karen believes in signs, connections, and even the spirits, but I don't. Yet things are happening that people outside of the village wouldn't know about. I reach for Karen to know she's with me and I'm happy she's safe. I finally fall asleep.

Chapter 23

I find Karen alone in the kitchen, she's staring into her coffee cup, but looks up smiles. She sighs, "I do love you. I love your kind heart, and I know you want to be sure you have the right answers to this situation, but I do miss you."

"I know, and I love you."

"Yeah, but there are times when I'm not sure if I come in first or second to your love of being a cop."

"First. Always first."

"Sure! Whatever." Karen shakes her head.

"So, what would you like to do today?"

"Later let's go into the village and have a late lunch at O'Neil's."

Our quiet morning happens at home with Karen smiling and dancing in the kitchen with Hannah then time filled with games of Candyland and an animated movie filled with fairies and a princess.

The phone rings. Answering it, I hear Quinn talking about the results of the postmortem are in, "It appears to be suicide."

"Are you sure?" I'm caught off guard; I was convinced it was murder.

"I'll tell you what the M.E. told me. 'The victim had a ligature pattern running from the front to the back. This happens when a person hangs themselves because they're suspended by their neck with the entire weight of the body pulling downward. Also, he said he opened the neck and found no bruising, which would have been present if the victim had been strangled and then hung.'"

Rubbing my forehead, I can't believe it, "Is that all?"

"No. There were no signs of trauma anywhere on the body. No needle marks, punctures, or bruises. The victim had no markings that would indicate being physically restrained or subdued. The condition of the skin around the neck shows the injuries were not present prior to death. This indicates that hanging was the cause of death. Human flesh reacts differently after death. When a ligature is applied after death, the furrow is fairly even. The tissue is not being infused with blood. It's drier and more yellowish."

"My gut told me that it was too easy. That it was a murder made to look like a suicide to end the investigation. So, there was nothing in the report that appeared odd?"

Quinn pauses, "Not really, just that it's odd for a woman to commit suicide by hanging, but not unheard of. Also, there was a fair amount of barbiturates in her system, but again not unheard of. Per the M.E. many suicide victims use medication prior to the act so they don't back out. It doesn't seem as if anything was missed. Nothing under Fi's fingernails or any signs of a struggle."

Shaking my head, I say, "Hey, thanks for the call." I look up and Karen is smiling at me.

"Yay, yay, I know, seeing murder everywhere. I guess I was wrong this time. Let's just get some lunch."

As we walk into the village, Hannah chatters happily about how to see fairies and how she might bring one home.

We're the only people in the restaurant. Sean O'Neil offers us any table we'd like. We find one near the window and he hands us menus. As we are deciding what to eat, Mary O'Neil comes out of the kitchen and says, "It is good to see you all. Are you all enjoying your time in Ballyram?"

Eric and Megan nod with affirmative. I state, "It seems a bit slow today. Is it normal for this time of the year?"

"It's the off-season. Isn't it a tragedy about our little Fionnuala? So young she was to end her life," Mary states.

"We were all shocked by the news," I say.

"I'm not surprised at all that Fi would turn to suicide at her feelins' of rejection. She was seein' herself as the next Lady O'Connor, but alas, it wasn't meant to be. Her mother also used pills to end her life, but then Fionnuala hung herself. This is truly a sad time in the village."

Karen and I look at each and I can't resist asking, "I guess I don't understand what you mean."

"You wouldn't be knowin' the history of Fionnuala. She and my daughter, Nora, were best friends from when they were little on through school. After her mother's death, the poor girl was never the same. She became obsessed with her appearance and money. She seemed to be looking for love and acceptance, especially from men. Fionnuala spent a great deal of time at our house and I thought of her as a second daughter. She was a good friend to my Nora when Nora lost her father, me first husband, in a tragic accident."

"I'm sorry to hear of your loss," Karen states.

"Himself was a drinker and no good ever came out of a bottle. He was home drunk one night, slipped, and fell down the stairs and died from bleedin' in his head."

Now it's my turn, "I'm terribly sorry. That must have been awful for both you and Nora."

"It was, but Nora had good friends and I had this place to keep me busy. We both made it through. Have the Garda closed the case on Fionuala's death?"

I am always suspicious of other people's questions, but I say, "I'm not sure. That would be up to the police."

"Fionnuala was a sensitive child. It's still a shame and a tragic loss."

Not wanting to reveal my sources, I ask, "I believe you and your daughter found Fi after her first suicide attempt. Do you happen to remember if she left a suicide note at that time?"

"Who would be tellin' you that?" Mary asks. Her silvery grey curls seem to become pointed, and her hands twitch the apron over themselves.

"I'm sorry I don't remember. Is it true?

"More's the pity. Yes, it's true."

"And a note?" I know I'm pushing here, but it would be helpful to know.

Curtly Mary replies, "I'm not rememberin'. It was a long time ago and I was more worried about Finnuala at the time."

"Of course, you were. Good thing Fi had you and Nora," I state.

"Excuse me. I'll be gettin' to your lunch. Nice to see you all again." Mary returns to the kitchen with Sean right behind her.

"Way to go, Pops. Before you leave, you may have annoyed everyone in the village, Mom included," Eric comments.

Karen sighs and changes the subject to the kids' visit to Blarney Castle. We are happily exchanging our experiences when lunch arrives. Everyone settles into eating and offering bites of their selection. I have to admit Mary is an amazing cook.

After lunch, Karen, Eric, and Megan decide to do some grocery shopping. I take Hannah into Maeve's Gift Shop. Kathleen is behind the register today. No one else is in the store. Hannah is immediately drawn to the left-hand side of the store. Her eyes grow wide and she exclaims, "Poppa, fairies!!" and runs to the display.

I look at Kathleen, "I'm sorry about your sister's troubles."

Kathleen nods, but offers nothing more. Kathleen smiles brightly at Hannah, then leans down to speak to her and offers to introduce each fairy to her. Hannah nods enthusiastically. The first introduction is to the queen of the fairies as this is proper etiquette, according to Kathleen. Hannah curtseys. Next is the queen's court. Kathleen is very specific that each fairy has a name and individual qualities. Their abilities range from being able to sing, play certain instruments, or cast spells.

Hannah is mesmerized. Kathleen is kind and patient with Hannah and I know now what Karen saw in Kathleen. I start, "We would be honored if one of the fairies would come to live with Hannah. Would that be possible?"

Hannah's face glows, "I promise to be nice and share my room with her."

Kathleen leans into the display and whispers to the statues. Then she replies, "Maribel would love to go home with you, but you must promise that the other fairies can come and visit any time they wish."

Hannah nods and claps her hands with joy. Maribel is a fairy about five inches high, with red hair and an emerald green dress who is a wonderful dancer. Kathleen carefully removes Maribel from the display and places her in a gift box that resembles an Irish cottage. I pay for the statue and we leave the store. Hannah is holding the box as if it were a precious heirloom. We meet up with the rest of the family outside.

I explain that Maribel is coming home with us and the circumstances of the open invitation for fairies. Kathleen may be sensitive to her belief in fairies, but her fierce protection of the fairies' home still makes me wonder to what lengths she would go to protect them.

I suddenly look up and Karen is laughing at me.

"What?" I ask.

"You're sitting there, hyper-focusing on a case that is technically not yours and muttering to yourself."

"I know. It's the whole situation with Fi's death that's setting off my coppy senses."

"What do you think needs to happen next?"

I pause, look straight at Karen, and begin to smile, "I think we need a memorial service for Fi."

Karen tilts her head, "What?"

"A memorial service! Well, Fi is all alone and I can cast a wide net to see who tries to wiggle out. I'll come up with a list of people who need to be there. If I go in with Quinn and Fr. Kennedy, can we have it pulled together for the day after tomorrow?"

"Yeah, I think so. Where were you planning on holding this memorial service?"

"We can't do it at the Lamb and Ram or Foley's because of people's feelings toward one pub or the other. What about here?"

"So, we'd be host a memorial service for someone we barely knew?"

"Yes," I answer with optimism in my voice.

Karen holds up her hand, "Okay, I need a minute to think about this. It's bad enough that you want me in on this, but we're not involving the kids.

"Sure, but you will help, right?"

Karen sighs and shakes her head, "This is crazy. I don't think people are going to come. A lot of people in the village had issues with Fi. How do you think we're going to get them to show up?"

"I think if we put it to people the right way, even if they didn't like Fi, they'll show up as a sign of respect or a kindness. I'll clear the plan with Quinn tomorrow. Can you write out a list of people to contact? I might actually sleep tonight. I love this idea."

Karen rolls her eyes and replies sarcastically, "Yeah great!"

Chapter 24

The next morning, leaving the youngsters to a board game and talk of Hannah's fairy visitors, Karen and I hurry into the village. Karen worked up a simple menu last night and will start shopping as soon as Quinn is on board with the idea.

Once at the station, I explain to Quinn my idea, "I'll act as a waiter bringing you empty glasses to process and hold for evidence."

"Good thing I haven't officially closed the case," Quinn says as he winks and smiles.

In order for this service to go off as planned, I'll need to speak to people in person due to the limited time involved. My first stop is the lace shop. I'm lucky Kathleen is there without any customers.

Kathleen brightens up when she sees me, "How is the newest member of your family, Maribel, settling in?"

"Hannah and Maribel have become great friends."

Kathleen beams, "Brilliant."

I clear my throat, "My wife and I would like to invite you both to a memorial service that we're hosting for Fionnuala Lynch. We know she was all alone, and we'd like to do something to help Fi find some peace. There will also be light lunch. Can I count on you to attend?"

Kathleen begins shredding a tissue from her pocket, "That girl caused a fair amount of misery in this village during her lifetime.

I'm not sure we should be celebrating that."

"I'm not asking to celebrate that. I'm asking that the village come together to put Fi to rest and begin to heal."

Kathleen joins in, "It's the Christian thing to do. I'll attend."

I thank her and give her the time and place.

I head over to Harvey and Claire's store. When I give them my request, Claire's eyes flare wide with anger and she spits out, "Are you kidding? That bitch caused me nothing but grief."

"I appreciate what you're saying. However, I'm calling upon you as leaders in the village to set an example of how persons with class rise to occasions. Your presence will go a long way in putting this chapter in the village history to rest."

My flatter works on Claire's ego. She relaxes her shoulders and releases a deep breath, "You're right! People of our standing must be an example for those who struggle with social graces. You can count on both of us to be there."

Harvey nods in agreement. I'm sure he has had years of practice in agreeing with his wife.

I stop by the parish rectory to speak with Fr. Kennedy who welcomes me into his office.

"I know my wife and I are new in town, but we're planning a memorial service for Finnoula Lynch tomorrow at 1 p.m. at our cottage. Karen and I would love it if you could come."

"Brilliant. Aye, that's a mighty kind act you'll be doin'. I'll be there with a prayer for the occasion. Thank you for your act of kindness," replies Father Kennedy.

I feel a bit guilty deceiving him, but if there is a murderer in the village, they need to be caught and Fr. Kennedy is not in the deceiving business.

I proceed to coax other people in the village to attend, including Michael Foley, Ralph Santini, and Timothy Clarke. I use all my skills I learned as a hostage negotiator. In the end they all agree, if not reluctantly, to come. I also speak with Mary and Sean O'Neil as well as Nora O'Brien.

Karen and I return home, but I'm anxious for what tomorrow may bring. I can't seem to calm down enough for sleep, but when I do, I have a series of frightening dreams, most involving shots being fired by unknown people. I repeatedly wake up fearing for what might happen at the memorial. I'm up before the sun. I quietly make coffee for myself and attempt to settle in with my book when Hannah appears out of the bedroom.

"Good morning, Poppa. What are you doing?"

"Good morning. Nothin' much."

"Poppa, can we go for a walk and try to see the fairies' home in the woods? Can we?"

"It's still kinda dark out, but sure, we can try."

"Yay! I'll tell momma and dadda!"

"NO, no just quietly go in your room and find some clothes to wear. Your coat and shoes are out here."

A few minutes later we are walking down the road. Hannah is happily skipping ahead of me. "Hannah don't get too far ahead. I need to be able to see you."

"Okay."

Wisps of blue light flicker on and off trailing into the woods, I wonder of it's the Wil o' the Wisp, and that's when I notice an old truck stopped on the side of the road, lights off and no one inside.

"Hannah, I need you to stay close to me."

My coppy senses entice me to the car. The doors aren't locked, so I open the driver's side and look in. Nothing much, just something that looks like a surveyor's map. Who would be out at this time of the morning? The hood of the truck is slightly warm to the touch.

Looking up, I realize Hannah's gone, "Hannah? Hannah, where are you? Poppa can't see you. HANNAH!" In the distance the flickering blue lights continue as if lighting the way. Pure fear grips my body and mind. I can't seem to catch my breath. My chest feels constricted and my legs refuse to move as fast as I want them to. I'm chasing after the lights, but don't know why. "HANNAH! HANNAH, WHERE ARE YOU?" Hannah screams from within the forest. I run toward where I think the scream came from. I accelerate. About twenty feet away, the first light illuminates two figures, one much taller than the other. I see Hannah and Charles O'Leary. He's holding a metal rake with the tines pointed at my granddaughter. "STOP!" I yell.

Hannah turns and runs to me. O'Leary snaps his head in my direction, "Oye. She should know better than to follow the Wil o' the Wisps."

"What? What are you talking about?"

"Following the Wisps to god knows where can be dangerous. Who knows what evil is out on the land? Laird O'Connor took no mind and see what it did to him. As for that tart Fi, I'll say no more of her."

Hannah is behind me, crying, clinging to my leg as we back away, "Stay away from my granddaughter and stay away from my family. I'm warning you."

"I'm *warning you.* Stay off my land." He swings the rake in my direction. I'm able to duck my head in time and just miss being struck.

I grab Hannah's hand and we hurry toward the road. She sobs and tries to catch her breath. "I'm sorry, Poppa. I thought the fairies wanted me to play with them in their secret garden. Don't tell momma or dadda. Please."

I pick Hannah up and assure her its fine. She clings to my neck the rest of the way, but I honestly don't remember the walk home. I'm sure of one thing, O'Leary has moved up on my list of most likely suspects. He certainly has enough anger to lash out violently.

Sitting at the kitchen table, I suddenly hear Karen say, "DAN."

"I'm sorry, what?"

"You haven't heard anything I've been talking about. You haven't moved or said a word since you and Hannah came back from your walk an hour ago. Is everything okay?"

"Yes, fine. I'm distracted about the Memorial today, that's all. No big deal" *Except I need to find out more about The Angry Farmer. His wife might be nice, but not him. The fear of losing his home and lifestyle is motive for murder.*

"The picture. What about the picture?" Karen asks.

"Karen, what picture are you talking about?"

Hands on her hips, she sighs, and drops her shoulders, "A picture of Fi for the table at the Memorial. We talked about having a picture, but all we have is the one of her and Laird O'Connor from the night of his party. Think that'll be okay if I crop the picture to just have Fi?"

The 'tart' and 'himself' forever bound together in my mind. Why can't I seem to get this statement off my mind? Random guess or what does O'Leary really know?

"Dan, you have to say your answer out loud. Thinking it doesn't help me any."

I wave my hand in a dismissive manner, "Yeah, I'm sure that'll be fine."

"Okay. I'm gonna make a quick breakfast for us and then the kids could take a walk, while we start setting up.

If O'Leary is the killer, then everything being done today is just to eliminate a number of other suspects because I didn't think to invite the O'Learys.

In a little over an hour, Karen has food set out and I have glasses ready for drinks. Quinn has his fingerprint kit, DNA swabs, and evidence bags set up in the laundry room. The plan is for him to collect glasses and process the evidence. Karen goes about decorating a small table with the picture of Finnoula and a candle. Eric, Megan and Hannah have decided to take a ride around the county during the memorial service. Shortly after 1 p.m., people start to arrive. Fr. Kennedy thanks us again for our generous Christian thoughts and action. I have ruled him out as a suspect in either case due to lack of motive to kill either victim. Next to arrive are Michael Foley and his uncle. He's tearful and clearly upset. He's a suspect because he was in love with Fi. He blames Brian for stealing her from him, then dumping her and returning to his wife. Michael believes Brian's action deeply hurt Fi. Shortly after them, Ralph arrives and thanks me for including him in the service. He had issues with Laird O'Connor. Ralph believes the Laird cheated him when Ralph bought the coffee shop's building and Fi, who dumped him when she found out Ralph wasn't rich.

Sean and Mary O'Neil along with Nora arrive. Curiously none of them take an interest in Fi's photo. In fact, they stand across the room and with their backs to it. What's that about,

I wonder? Brian and Diedre also attend. Michael Foley shoots a menacing look at Brian. Brian averts his eyes and maneuvers Diedre to the opposite side of the room. Kathleen arrives next.

I'm pleased and say, "Welcome. Thank you for coming."

Karen wanders around the room making sure people know to help themselves to the lunch.

The door swings open with a loud bang and there stands Claire Clarke, whose dramatic entrance causes some people jump, but everyone turns their head to look. She's wearing red with a significant V plunge in the front. Not at all appropriate for a memorial service. As if to read my mind, Claire announces, "Let's get this party started!" She appears joyous. A burden lifted or a rival dispatch.

Harvey and Claire's brother-in-law Tim follows quietly behind her and blushing a deep red; he quickly closes the door behind them. I put on my best poker face and welcome them. "Be sure to help yourself to the food and again thank you for coming."

Fr. Kennedy stands and asks us to say a blessing before everyone begins eating. People stop talking and lower their heads. Fr. Kennedy makes the sign of the cross, "Bless us, Dear Lord, during this troubling time. Shine your light on our young soul Fionnuala. Grant her a place in Heaven. Amen."

All but Claire respond, "Amen." People return to talking and resume eating.

As the memorial progresses, Quinn walks around with a tray for people to put their empty glasses on and takes them into the back room where he dusts each one for prints, swabs the rim for DNA, and finishes by bagging and tagging each glass with the person's name and date they were collected. A master list is created with the names of everyone from whom samples were taken.

Quinn maintains all of the samples and places each one in a locked storage box. My gut has convinced me that the prints on Fi's suicide note and/or the DNA on the rope will belong to someone in town. Now Quinn and I just need to prove it.

Once they finish their meals, nobody lingers. The cottage is empty in under two hours of the first guest arriving. Karen, Quinn and I breathe a sigh of relief.

"We have a full count," Quinn reports. "Each person who attended the service has provided a sample of fingerprints and DNA. Brilliant. All we need to do now is wait for analysis from the crime lab."

This is the worst part. There is little Quinn and I can do. We cannot move forward with an arrest at this time. Our best tactic is to become invisible, so Quinn's supervisors don't remember the case remains open.

With drinks in hand, Karen, Quinn and I sit at the kitchen table and debrief on the day. We eat the remains of the lunch. Eric, Megan and Hannah arrive home shortly after the service ends and they take leftovers to enjoy in front of the T.V. Karen has a dish of fortune cookies leftover from take-out orders in the middle of the table.

As we finish, Karen grabs a fortune cookie, "'Your dearest dream will come true.' I guess that means this case *WILL* be solved with the evidence you collected today, and you'll be a husband again!"

Quinn reads his, "'You are capable, competent, creative, careful. Prove it.' I can hope, at least."

I can't help but laugh at mine, "'Keep your plans secret for now.' How true, because if this doesn't work out, I'm not sure what the next step will be!" Quinn and Karen are laughing with me. Quinn excuses himself to go home. Karen and I join the kids in front of the T.V. for a quiet end to this day.

Chapter 25

I'm up before anyone else and decide on an early morning walk. The ground under my feet is soft and muddy from an overnight rain. I sink into the earth and it clings to my shoes. The air is damp and thick. I work to draw deep breaths. I'm walking nowhere in particular. I just need time. Time to revisit the memorial from yesterday. Going over what I saw or heard or maybe didn't. Brian Flynn was reluctant to give Quinn his glass, but why? Claire Clarke didn't order a drink for quite a while after she arrived, yet had said, "Let's get this party started." I caught Sgt. Foley trying to sneak into the laundry room. He said he was looking for the bathroom, which was clearly evident on the other side of the room. Frustrated, I walk back home.

I enter the house and Karen is putting her jacket on. "I was beginning to worry; you've been gone a long time."

I shake my head, "A lot to think about. I'm just to sort out this case."

"I'm going into the village. Yesterday when I saw Ralph Santini at the Memorial, it struck me that maybe Mary's secret ingredient didn't come from Doyle's grocery store, but maybe it's from the Second Byte health food store. I was right! Ralph said that he orders mango syrup by the case for Mrs. O'Neil, so I'm going to buy a jar and mixed it in. I have the crust done already, so when I get back it shouldn't take me long to make."

"Would you like me to go with?" I ask.

"No, I'll be home soon."

Karen heads off and I settle in on the couch with my book. I must have fallen asleep for a couple hours because I wake to the smell of homemade pie. Karen has again attempted to recreate Mary O'Neil's Very Fruity Pie. I'm not sure I can force myself to eat another slice.

Karen confidentially announces, "I think I got it right this time.

I force myself to feign interest, "Really, so you think the mango syrup is the 'secret' ingredient?"

"Here's to hoping. So, when it's cooled would you try a slice?"

I put on my best smile. I owe Karen for her support while I've been investigating the murders.

Reluctantly I take the first bite, but I'm pleasantly surprised. I admit, "You're right. This is nearly a perfect recreation. Good job!"

"Yes! I knew I could do it! I'll have to tease Mary that I've learned her secret," Karen winks.

I comment, "No offense but can we not have pie for a while? I'd eat any other dessert like cake or brownies."

Karen laughs, "I agree. No more pie for a while."

I let out a sigh of relief. It has only taken eight attempts.

Karen grins at me, "I've got her now." Karen calls Mary and announces that she has discovered her secret and would like to discuss it with her. Karen leaves to walk to the O'Neil's a little before 3 p.m.

Ten minutes later, I receive a call from Quinn, "The plan worked! We have a match to the prints on the suicide note and the blood on the rope. Both of them are from Ballyram residents."

"Both of them? You mean that there's more than one donor?"

"Yes, and they're a married couple. I don't want to go into too much detail here on the phone. Would you be able to come to the constabulary to discuss the results and then we'll go confront the suspects."

"I'll be right over." I feel vindicated that the formerly unidentified prints do belong to someone in the village and a married couple, at that. I'm sad to think it could be our original suspects of Brian and Diedre Flynn, but then there's Claire and Harvey Clarke. I'm anxious to find out the truth, so I leave for the station immediately.

While I am savoring my victory, I hope Karen is savoring hers with Mary. My mind wanders to images of Karen and Mary sitting in her kitchen with tea and a fabulous dessert. I laugh to think it could be a slice of 'Very Fruity Pie,' but I'm happy for Karen's success.

At the station Quinn meets me at the front desk. Once he informs me who the samples belong to, my worst fears are realized. I reach for my phone, but it suddenly rings. As I answer it, I can hear Karen's voice, "Peanut butter and jelly."

The word "Hello" never reaches my lips because I hear my wife using our code for danger. There's no time to waste.

I hear Mary saying, "Why do Americans always talk so loudly? You're just rude!"

I'm out the door in seconds, running faster than my bad knees like, but this is for Karen. The O'Neil's Bed and Breakfast is four or five blocks from the station. Quinn follows, asking 'What's wrong?' The voices continue from the cell phone held hard in my hand. *Keep talking*, I think. *Keep talking*.

Mrs. O'Neil is spitting, "Peanut butter and jelly! What a stupid thing to say. No! That little bitch kills Himself and gets away with it. Now *you've* learned me secret and it starts again."

"Finnoula *told* you that she killed Lord O'Connor?" Karen asks.

"Oh yes, Fi felt she could admit it to me when I confronted her. She said it was one murderer to another; knowin' that I would have to keep her secret for her to keep mine. Just in case she left you a bouquet of Marigolds and Yew branches with the note to 'Leave it alone', but that husband of yours couldn't." Mary spats out, "Fi was a greedy bitch. She tried to say that nothin' had changed in our arrangement."

Karen pipes in "Who'd you kill?"

"What do you mean who'd I kill? Me first husband! He sat around the pub with his mates drinking up the profits I earned. He was a mean and lazy drunk. So, one night he had a convenient 'accident' falling down the stairs.

"Fi figured out the accident wasn't so accidental, so that was your 'secret.'"

"She was a little snoop and thief." Mary continues, "I was prescribed a blood thinner, Coumadin they called it, for a blood clot issue in me leg. I chose not to take it all. Do ye know how many times a cook nicks her knuckles or scrapes her fingertips? Them doctors don't know, or they never would've prescribe it. I had it in me kitchen spice cabinet and chose to 'spice' my husband's whiskey. One night he came home drunk again and I was waiting for him at the top of the stairs. It didn't take much to push him down."

Karen continues to stall, "No one suspected that it wasn't an accident?"

"There were rumors in the village after his death due to the coroner's remark on the extent of my husband's bleeding." Mary sniffs, "Called it some rubbish, some subdural hematoma. However, Sgt. Foley is lazy. He blamed me husband's drinking for his thin blood and the coroner agreed. That was exactly as I hoped."

Karen gasps, "So you thought you had gotten away with murder. That is until Fi found out."

"When she was over here, she'd look in drawers and cabinets. When Fi saw the pills, she thought she could sell them for some fast cash, but then she learned that Coumadin doesn't have a street value. However, Miss Smarty Pants Fi figured out what happened. She threatened to go to the Garda. It was just a few dollars at first, but then more and more."

"You couldn't put up with that anymore, so Fi would need to have a crisis of conscience and commit suicide with some assistance from you."

"Exactly! I just wanted a quiet life, with a few dollars to spend and a man who cares for me. Now what to do with you?" Drumming her fingers, Mary pauses, "Your tea is ready. And you'll be drinkin' it."

"I'm sorry I put you through the trouble of pulling out that pretty china tea cup and everything, but I don't think I'm really in the mood for tea. Thank you for the offer, though."

I hear the venom in Mary's voice through the phone, "Shut your mouth, you stupid woman. I'll have to insist that you drink it, deary. We can't be havin' nobody knowin' the truth."

"Sean, why are you standing there, in the living room doorway with a knife in your hand? What's going on? I see that both doorways are blocked. I take it there is something in the tea that won't agree with me," Karen snaps.

"It's a special tea, brewed from the leaves of a foxglove plant," Mrs. O'Neil offers.

Karen replies, "I know plants and that would be a raw form of digitalis that's used in the treatment of heart issues."

Mary sneers, "Always so smart! Yes dear, it'll look as if you had a heart attack, you poor thing. Your heart is already beating hard, I'm sure."

I'm sure Karen's heart is beating hard, but mine is galloping.

"How are you going to explain two deaths in your home?" Karen coyly asks.

"I'm not. Your body will be found somewhere else, perhaps in the woods of Charles O'Leary. It'll be the result of an argument with that angry, little man," she says, and I can hear Mary's laugh.

I hit the door with my shoulder, Quinn is right behind me. I see an arc of brown liquid as Karen's cup hits the floor. Sean moves toward us.

Mary looks at Karen, who produces her cell phone held in a shaking hand.

In wide eyed amazement, "I didn't know a thing," Sean says.

"What? You knew everything," his wife shouts. "You knew it all!"

Quinn takes a step in front of me, "Sean and Mary, I am arresting you on suspicion of murder."

Karen looks at both of us, "What did you two do, crawl here? I thought you'd never show up. I was running out of things to say to stall them."

I snap back, "You should say 'I love you, and thank you!'"

Karen beams, "Looks as if I caught the murderers."

"I've often said you should have been the cop in the family."

Quinn proceeds to 'Caution' the O'Neils and calls for assistance in transporting the prisoners back to the station.

Late afternoon, Karen, Quinn, Brian and Deidre Kelly, and I are sitting at a table at the Lamb and Ram. The pub is closed tonight. We're all drinking coffee.

Brian is staring at his coffee cup, "I've been sober since my arrest. I'm working the AA program. I owe all of you so much for your belief in my innocence. I'll do me best to have you be proud of me."

Deidre leans toward him and squeezes his shoulder. Her hair is tidy and her face softly beaming.

I ask, "Will you be able to stay sober owning and working in a pub?"

"I'm working on the idea that I'm powerless over alcohol. Just one step of many, I'll need to take, if Deidre will help me."

Deidre nods affirmation and adds, "I was talking with Kathleen about how surprised I was that Mary O'Neil was a murderer when Kathleen pointed out that the name Mary, can mean '*Sea of Bitterness.*'"

I look at Quinn and ask, "What about Mary? Have you had any luck having her confess to Fi's death?"

Quinn shakes his head, "The problem is getting her *to stop* talking. After booking her, I was in an interview room with her for two hours. There's a great deal of pent up rage and frustration in her. She said that Fi's arrogance at thinking she had gotten away with Laird O'Connor's death enraged her and that's when she decided to plan Fi's death. Mary arranged to meet at Fi's home for a larger pay out, and she'd bring the sleeping pills and a bottle of Fi's favorite red wine. She dropped the pills into Fi's wine. It wasn't a very original plan, but effective. When Fi was unconscious, Mary had Sean help her stage the scene of Fi's supposed suicide by hanging.

I couldn't resist, "What about Fi's suicide note?"

"Mary brought it with her."

"I had a feeling that she was lying when I asked about a note from Fi's suicide attempt as a teenager and she said she couldn't remember if there was one or not."

Quinn shrugs, "She's is a bit of a hoarder and was never able to part with the note. She realized it would come in handy now."

"What about Sean?" I ask.

"He's being charged as an accessory to murder. His DNA was on the rope. He failed to calculate how heavy Fi's body would be when he dropped her over the balcony railing." Quinn grins. "They always do forget that bit about 'dead weight.' The rope slipped through his hands. As he grabbed it, it tore through the rubber gloves he was wearing and cut into his hand. It was too late to get another length of rope. The best he could hope for is that the investigators would accept the scene as a suicide and not test the rope. Apparently, he guessed wrong with you on the case."

"That's some very nice police work with three murders solved and two murderers exposed."

Quinn laughs and says, "Brilliant. I appreciate your assistance in this. It helped to have the voice of experience to check with. I learned a great deal about investigative techniques."

"You're going to make a good detective. Besides I don't think I did much on this case. Ouch!" I instinctively rub my leg where Karen has kicked me under the table.

Everyone laughs.

Karen rolls her eyes and says, “Whatever.”

And I think that one of the best parts of this is that we can go back to the cottage together. Karen’s safe, and there’s time for family and a real Irish vacation to begin. Because of course, I’m in love with my life and *I’m retired.*

CPSIA information can be obtained
at www.ICGtesting.com
Printed in the USA
BVHW09s0245290818
525384BV00001B/3/P